Death by Surfboard

by

Susie Black

The Holly Swimsuit Mystery Series

Death by Surfboard

Cover Art by *The Wild Rose Press, Inc.*

The Wild Rose Press, Inc.
PO Box 708
Adams Basin, NY 14410-0708
Visit us at www.thewildrosepress.com

Publishing History
First Edition, 2023
Trade Paperback ISBN 978-1-5092-4668-7
Digital ISBN 978-1-5092-4669-4

The Holly Swimsuit Mystery Series
Published in the United States of America

Andy leaned over the pier railing and yelled, "Holy mackerel! Old man, you've hooked you a surfer!"

Pop and I gave Andy a pitying you-must-be-crazy-or-something glance. Pop summoned a burst of energy, hauled the rod over his left shoulder, and gave an enormous tug on the line.

My eyes bugged as the battered, wet-suited body of Jack Tyne, still attached by his surf leash to his surfboard, flopped unceremoniously onto the pier.

Pop, Andy, and I stared at one another. As long-time pier locals, we'd seen a lot of crazy things, but nothing compared to this.

We inched closer to the crumpled body, hopelessly entangled in the fishing line for any sign of life. Andy cautiously toed his faded deck shoe on the left leg of the prone body. "Is the guy dead?"

Since Jack hadn't so much as twitched, Pop angled his leathery face closer to Jack's pasty grayish kisser to see if he was as dead as he looked. Pop leaned in and passed a hand over Jack's mouth. Pop took a breath, and Siggie barked when the old man jumped back as though he'd been burned by a cattle prod.

Andy looked at the old man and joked. "Whatssamatta? The guy's breath that bad?"

The old man pointed a crooked index finger at Jack's pummeled body. "Poor bastard doesn't have any breath at all. He's dead as a doornail."

Naturally, I burst out laughing.

Praise for Susie Black

"Holly Schlivnik will never take no for an answer, much to the enjoyment of the reader."
~ *Ellen Byerrum, author Crime of Fashion series*

"A real mystery escape!"
~ *CeeCee James, author*
Flamingo Realty Mystery Series

"Susie Black's latest mystery is full of unique, quirky characters."
~ *Charlotte Rains Dixon,*
author Emma Jean's Bad Behavior

"Foul play is a-foot in this fashion-filled cozy mystery series."
~ *Melissa Bourbon, Author of the Magical*
Dressmaking Series

"The Holly Swimsuit Mysteries are a guaranteed fun romp."
~ *Kim Hunt Harris,*
author Trailer Park Princess Mysteries

"I highly recommend it, and am looking forward to the next one!"
~ *Dianne Harman,*
USA Today Bestselling Author

"Holly is a hoot! This is one humorous cozy mystery you won't want to miss."
~ *Nancy J. Cohen, Bad Hair Day Mystery*

Dedication

This book is lovingly dedicated to the most influential person in my writing career, my nana. If there is an inheritable gene for storytelling, mine came from my mother's mother. My nana should have been a writer. No one could tell a story like her. When reporting back to her siblings on the plot of the serialized silent film she'd seen, Nana would take her time, slowly build up to the cliffhanger and pause right before the finale. Talk about pacing and how to build tension to the finale? Nana had it down pat.

The designated town crier, Nana's weekly letters to the family were more like a newsletter. A date with her friends at the movies? After reading Nana's letter, I was in the seat next to her and could write a decent review based on her commentary. Her descriptions were so detailed and rich, that if she was describing a meal, I could smell the wafting aroma and taste the food.

Out of sentimentality or maybe a sixth sense that someday I'd need them, I kept every one of those letters. Like Nana, they were strong-willed and hearty, surviving dogs, a child, countless moves, several major earthquakes, and a devastating house fire.

I had no formal creative writing training when I decided to write my first manuscript. I had a story to tell, but no clue how to tell it. I instinctively pulled the carefully wrapped packets of letters out of the storage box and re-read every one of them.

I could picture Nana at the dining room table writing the letters. I heard her voice inside my head speaking to me. My long-gone, full-service nana had given me all the tools I needed. I re-packed the letters, started to write, and thanks to Nana, I never stopped. I kept Nana's story-telling skills in mind while writing The Holly Swimsuit Mystery Series books. Somewhere in the great beyond, Nana is smiling her approval. Thanks a bunch, Nana. I am on my way to a successful writing career, and I owe it all to you.

Chapter One

Mermaid Swimwear CEO David Workman's page blared on the intercom at the same time I dialed the head guy's extension. He bellowed, "Holly Schlivnik, call two-one-one! Holly, two-one-one!" And the familiar twists of my gut turned at the sound of his voice. It begged the question, why? Nothing good. This is not a man who calls you into his office to say good morning. Yet I'd been mid-dial for his extension, and he'd merely beaten me to it. Shaking off the unsettling clench of foreboding that gripped my heart every time the boss paged me proved impossible. Old habits die hard.

Before going any further, let me introduce myself and explain my role in this tale. I am Holly Schlivnik, president of the juniors, kids, and private label divisions of Mermaid Swimwear.

When Rob Bachmann sold Ditzy Swimwear where I'd served as Vice President of Sales, the new owners were not my cup of tea, and I chose to move on. My colleague and friend Queenie Levine recommended me to David to run the new Mermaid juniors and kids divisions. The additional responsibility of private label became mine after Gracie Fernando, my first boss at Mermaid, got fired. Although I fought it tooth and nail, David recently concluded he put too much on my plate and gave me the choice of relinquishing either the juniors and kids divisions or the private label.

I made my way to David's office with the caution of a bomb squad. I took a deep breath, knocked twice on David's open door, and entered his office. David is not keen for idle chitchat, so I came right to the point. "Funny you paged me." I took a seat across from David at his massive mahogany desk and hoped for the best. "I was mid-dial calling your extension when you paged."

Fiftyish, always impeccably dressed, average height David Workman worked hard at maintaining his lean build. Set behind professorial tortoiseshell glasses, David's intelligent brown eyes never miss much. David arched a brow.

I smiled tightly and continued. "I've made my decision as to which division I want to keep…"

My internal antennae buzzed to life when he interrupted. "I paged you for the same reason." My stomach dropped to my toes with the speed of a runaway elevator at his imperious wave. "Effective immediately, you are no longer in charge of the juniors and kids divisions."

Controlling my tongue has never been one of my strong suits. My lips let the words escape before my brain stopped my foot from inserting itself into my mouth. I held my hands up in the air as if I'd been robbed. In a way, it was one and the same. "Whoa. Hold on a darned minute. You told *me* to *choose* which division to give up. Why pull the rug out from under me twice? First, you're making me give up something I want to keep. Now you take back the choice of which one to give up. Why are you doing this? Doesn't it even matter to you which one I'd want to keep?"

David regarded me over the rim of his eyeglasses and put me in my place. "I owe you no explanation, but in the spirit of fairness, I will. The juniors and kids divisions are thriving, and the private label division is struggling. The obvious choice is for you to focus all your efforts on fixing the private label division since the other category is in good shape and easily handed off to someone else."

And *this* is supposed to placate me? As if. I jutted my jaw. "Am I some sort of plumber?"

David laughed out loud. "No, but right now Harvey and the board swear you walk on water. Truth be told, Harvey questioned taking any category away from you."

I leaned over the desk. "So why are you? You're punishing me for doing too good a job." I gave him the stink eye. "Do I get a raise if I screw up enough?"

David put his hands out in supplication. "Take this as the compliment it is meant to be. You started from ground zero and performed so admirably that the category you developed is now worthy of standing on its own. We need you to focus on private label. It's a business we've put a lot of effort into, with not much to show for it. It's too big a business to walk away from, and the profit margins are too volatile to leave in the hands of someone we don't trust. You're the person we trust." A combination of disappointment and disapproval pursed his thin lips. "So, you'd chosen to keep juniors and kids. I'm rather surprised."

I gave him a sly grin. "Actually, I'd chosen to keep the private label division."

Not the answer he expected. He sputtered with the cadence of an engine running out of gasoline. "S-So w-why t-the a-attitude? D-Do y-you e-enjoy g-giving m-me c-crap?"

Duh.

My reply snapped with the crack of a whip. "I'm pissed you decided for me and for not trusting me to make the right choice."

David smiled, and his apology went all the way to his eyes. "You're right. I apologize. I never doubted you'd make the right choice, but I couldn't take the chance."

His line of reasoning made no sense, but debating the point? Why bother? I stood no chance of winning this argument. Nonetheless, David understood the concept of logic. "I assume fashion juniors and kids go to the new person, but not in the private label?"

He pushed his eyeglasses to the tip of his nose and smirked. "Need I remind you the first three letters in the word assumption are ASS?"

I blushed from head to toe.

David clucked his tongue. "Juniors and kids are now a completely independent category under one umbrella and separate president, irrespective of price point."

Undaunted, I kept at it. Persistence is my middle name. "You're ignoring a continuity issue."

I might be selling, but he wasn't buying. David gave me a nice try but no dice grin. "Not your concern. Believe me, there will be more programs to work on in missy and plus-sized private label, and not enough hours in the day to produce them."

I spun my mental Rolodex and took the tour of potential in-house candidates. Not a single name stood out. "No one is promotable in the company, so I guess you're hiring from out in the market. Since I come from the junior market, it makes sense for me to assist in the vetting process. Do you want a more narrowed or a wider list of potential candidates? If you're not keen on the candidates I recommend, I'll poll my buyers for additional names."

David glanced aside, chagrined. "You're right. There is no one to promote internally. We went into the industry and hired someone already."

The slap of the betrayal hit me as hard as though I'd been struck. On some level, I had been. I spat out the words as if they were watermelon seeds. "Then I *guess* you don't need my input." David either chose to ignore my sarcasm or missed it. I took a step back from the edge of corporate oblivion and went for a more conciliatory tone. "Who's taking over the division?"

David squirmed in his seat and found something fascinating to study on the ceiling. "I'd rather not say who we went with at this time."

I gave him an industrial-strength eye roll. "It's a state secret? Come on, David. We're on the same team, remember?"

David pursed his lips into a funnel. "Yeah, you're right. It's no secret, and everyone will find out soon enough. We hired Jack Tyne and signed a licensing agreement with a surf line called GOOFYFOOT Jack recommended."

If not for swimwear being such a small industry, I wouldn't know Jack Tyne from a Jack in the Box. We didn't run in the same circles, but some jaw-dropping Jack Tyne stories circulated the market. They gave the guy a sleazy enough reputation that should have scared off all potential employers from considering Tyne for any position. But David Workman is one who rarely listens to any voice except the one inside his head. So, it was no big surprise that he hired Jack. I mentally channeled God's assistant in charge of keeping a poker face and prayed for divine intervention.

David glanced at his watch as though waiting for Jack to join us. I half expected Jack to be standing outside David's office listening for his stage cue. I tried not to choke on my words. I focused on keeping my voice from shrieking as I croaked with the rasp of a bullfrog. "Has he already started?"

David consulted his day planner. "No. He'll complete the human resources paperwork on Monday. We're formally introducing Jack to the executives at the management meeting next Wednesday. Start gathering all the juniors and kids reports, samples, and cost sheets and put everything into Jack's office. Harvey will give you the office Jack will be using." David glanced at his watch again to indicate the end of the meeting. "Anything else we need to discuss?"

My nana's sage advice said to always leave 'em laughing. "Other than that, Mrs. Lincoln, how did you enjoy the play?"

Chapter Two

I snapped the leash onto my standard poodle/psychiatrist Siggie's collar as the fire-orange sun slipped into the cerulean blue Pacific. I gave my pooch the lowdown on the David situation as we crossed Admiralty Way. We walked west on Washington Street, heading two blocks east of the beach to meet Queenie at Pasta at the Pier. A popular local hangout, the cozy bistro offered an outdoor, pet-friendly patio featuring a spectacular ocean view. As we approached the restaurant, I asked, "So, Sigmund, do I tell David he hired a slimeball or keep my mouth shut?" Siggie turned his big head sideways and said, "WOOF." I sighed with resignation. "I can't see how."

****

That we'd finished dinner and Queenie failed to mention a word about my meeting with David was nothing short of miraculous. Little snuck past the megaphone of the mart. Telephone, telegraph, tell Queenie. Cable news? Ha! No match for Queenie Levine. I finished off my Chardonnay and dipped my head. "I'm surprised you haven't said a word about the big news yet."

Queenie cocked a brow. "Big news?"

Alert the media. This was a first. "David said I've got too much on my plate."

She narrowed her eyes. "Am I waiting for a punch

line?"

I sighed. "No. There isn't one. But he's making me give up either juniors and kids or private label."

Queenie wrinkled her forehead. "So, I still see no problem. I'd be dancing in the street if he took back some of my responsibilities." She widened her eyes. "The rat cut your salary."

I frowned. "No. On the contrary. He said reducing my responsibilities is a compliment to my success."

Queenie scrunched her nose. "Ok, so why are you upset?"

I puffed the air out with my cheeks. "I'm being punished for doing too good a job. David magnanimously threw me a bone and allowed me to choose which division to give up. I made a decision, but before I had the chance to tell him what I decided, he decided for me and took juniors and kids back."

Queenie's eyes bugged. "Come on. You'd *actually* chosen to keep juniors and kids over private label?"

I shook my head. "No. *Actually* I decided to give juniors and kids up."

Queenie gave me the deer in the headlights. "So, I still see no problem. You made the same decision as him."

I slapped the table hard enough for Siggie to WOOF from his perch under my feet. "Do you people consult one another for comments? David said the same thing. The *problem is* I'm pissed he chose for me after telling me I could make the choice and for not trusting me to make the right decision on my own."

Queenie shook her head and blew out a pitying sigh. "Welcome to the world according to David Workman, kiddo. So, who is he gonna get to take juniors and kids?"

Her eyes grew as big as the coaster under her scotch. "Double crap on a cracker. No one else at Mermaid except *me* has any junior experience." She puckered her lips as though she had bitten into a grapefruit wedge. "If he's planning to shove it on me, he's got another thing coming. I need more on my plate like I need a bigger tush. He can double my salary. I'm still not doing it."

I rolled my eyes. "Untwist your panties. He's gone into the market and already hired someone."

She hoisted her glass of scotch and toasted the news. "Thank God." She reached under the table and gave Siggie an apologetic love scratch. "Present company excluded, Sigmund, but as long as it's not me, Rex the wonder dog can take it. Who'd you recommend? I hope you gave David Sonia Wilson's name." Queenie smiled evilly. "Imagine all the fun with three of us pushy broads ganging up on David? He'd never stand a chance."

I smiled sardonically. "You're getting too far ahead of yourself. David didn't ask for my help. Despite being unfamiliar with the juniors and kids markets, he still managed to find this one all on his own."

Queenie grinned and wiggled her brows. "At least you won't be held responsible if the person flames out." She frowned. "Nah. With our David? Not a chance. He'd point the finger at anyone but himself. Who got the nod?"

I struggled not to gag at the words. "He hired Jack Tyne, a gold medal slime ball. The word is he's an opportunistic fast talker who makes wild promises to worm into positions he's not qualified to fill."

Queenie reminded me of my nana as she tapped an index finger on her nose. "Jack Tyne, Jack Tyne. The name is familiar, but I can't place it."

I snapped my fingers. "You remember him. He's the guy who replaced Ronnie Schwartzman at Clothing Concepts after Ronnie was arrested for murdering Angela Wellborn."

"Oh yeah." She smirked. "This is a marriage made in Heaven. David finally met his match." She pursed her lips. "Our vaunted leader is a slug, but he's not an idiot. He wouldn't hire the guy without doing *some* due diligence. And this gem's background?"

I said, "He started at United Apparel running their juniors and kids divisions."

Queenie drummed her spoon to a beat on her shot glass. "If Jack Tyne worked for Milton, he has some skills. I worked for Milton at the beginning of my career. Milton eats incompetents for breakfast."

I said, "Jack's bounced around. He's been at Clothing Concepts for a few seasons. I guarantee you that no one voluntarily quits Clothing Concepts to come to Mermaid. Either Jack got fired, or he got the sniff his days were numbered and beat Martin Decker to the punch. David still hired him, so it doesn't seem like the boss did any due diligence."

Queenie ran her little finger around the rim of the shot glass. "I'll bet David thinks if Jack's good enough for Milton and Martin, he's good enough for Mermaid. So, he saw no need to ask around." Queenie batted her eyes. "You tell David any of this?"

I shook my head. "Not yet. I'll make some calls and confirm the stories before I say anything to David."

Queenie breathed a sigh of relief. "Thank heavens for small favors. My advice is you do absolutely nothing but keep a smile on your face and your big mouth shut. If David wanted your opinion, he'd ask for it. Since he didn't, do not offer him any advice, as it will not be appreciated. It'll come back and bite you on the butt. David is convinced no one is as sharp as him. Don't do anything to contradict him. If Jack Tyne is a dog, let David get bitten."

I reached under the table and gave my boy a love scratch behind his ears. "In case you're curious, you and Siggie are on the same page. But I'd never forgive myself if I had important information and failed to pass it along. They say the truth will never hurt you."

Queenie shook her head, and her hair whipped around like a wet dog drying off. "Nosiree. Not with our boss. David doesn't want the truth. He wants you to tell him what he wants to hear. He won't appreciate your concern for the company's welfare. Your intentions may be the best, but the road to hell is paved by them. Yours will get you kicked to the unemployment line, while Jack Tyne is sitting pretty in his new office."

Taking advice? As if. Never been one of my strong suits.

****

David slammed a fist on his desk so hard the crystal paperweight flew off and bounced onto the carpet and across the room. He growled through clenched teeth. "An unauthorized survey of retailers' opinions of a co-worker? Ordinarily, pulling a stunt this unprofessional gets you fired on the spot. You're lucky we need you, or you'd be out the door." He waved his index finger under my nose for emphasis in case I missed the message. "If you utter so much as one word of your alleged information to anyone, you *will* be gone. Have I made myself clear?"

Either I had a career death wish, or he'd pissed me

off to the point beyond caring. Toss a coin. I snarled. "Crystal." I looked David in the eye. "Funny, I never pegged you as a yes-man." No one with a brain ever talked so brazenly to David Workman. Was I still employed? As the guy in the movie said, frankly, my dear, I don't give a damn. David stared wide-eyed, either astonished or respectful. It didn't matter which. I was beyond caring what he thought. I didn't give him the chance to either fire me or reply to me. It took every ounce of control not to slam it behind me as I stomped out his office door.

For the next few days, things stayed pretty frosty between David and me. Our interactions were reduced to a curt nod to one another in the hall. At the end of the week, since no one escorted me out of the building with my stuff in a carton, miraculously, I managed to dodge the unemployment line.

Chapter Three

The following Wednesday morning, a definite air of curiosity permeated David's office as the Mermaid executives took their places around the conference table. A GOOFYFOOT surfboard leaned against a wall, and GOOFYFOOT goody bags covered David's desk. All eyes were glued to a conspicuously empty chair at the head of the conference table. David's. The rest of the executive staff arrived on time. We'd catch hell for being late. So, where was the boss?

The office door blew open, and preppy David Workman marched in dressed in full GOOFYFOOT regalia. In his rash guard, board shorts, matching deck shoes, logo cap, and sunglasses dangling around his neck on a logo lanyard, David resembled an over-the-hill surfer lost going to the beach. Stunned reactions buzzed around the conference table loud as a sawmill. I covered my palm over Queenie's mouth to prevent her from shrieking out loud.

David took his seat at the head of the conference table, and all chatter ceased. "Good morning, everyone. I am happy to start the meeting with some exciting news." He pointed to me, and I almost fell out of my chair. "Thanks to Holly's efforts in merely two seasons, the juniors and kids division went from nonexistence to having the highest finished gross margin in the history of the company. Holly's remarkable success reset the bar for the rest of us to meet. The growth rate and profitability of this division are so impressive that it is slated for extensive expansion. We've made it a separate division under its own umbrella. The new division has its own budget and independent team." He crowed with the pride of a rooster. "I am thrilled to announce the first expansion step we've taken is a licensing agreement with GOOFYFOOT, an iconic surf brand and the foundation of the industry for fifty years. To head the new juniors and kids division, we've been fortunate to persuade a seasoned surf industry veteran to join our team. It is my pleasure to introduce this highly respected swimwear expert, Jack Tyne." David looked over to his closed office door and called out, "Jack, come on in and meet everyone."

Right on cue, dressed from head to toe in the same GOOFYFOOT attire as David, Jack Tyne swooped into the meeting. He held his arms out for balance as though shooting the curl of a big wave. Tall, broad-shouldered, fortyish Jack Tyne had a sinewy, athletic physique. Jack dressed surfer style and strode into the room as though a conquering hero, but the guy appeared more like a circus clown. Given his light blue eyes, sun-bleached blonde hair, and perpetual tan, central casting couldn't conjure up an actor to better fill the role.

Queenie bit her lip to stifle a giggle. "OMG. Imagine if they both come to work dressed in such a ridiculous outfit every day?" She whispered, "They better not expect the rest of us to wear the same costume." She crossed her fingers into an X as though warding off a vampire. "Those low rider board shorts cut anyone my size in half."

David tipped his logo cap at Jack and gave him a

standing ovation. The executives surveyed the table and made a universal shrug as they all stood and clapped along. David and Jack joined hands and raised them in a Rocky Balboa victory salute. Good grief. Somebody, get the shovel.

Afraid I'd burst out laughing, I hid behind a computer report.

Queenie leaned over and dipped her head towards the two musketeers. "David's done everything but bow and scrape. Next, he'll kiss this clown's ass." Queenie's deep voice carried. I elbowed her in the ribs to cut the commentary as I caught David's glare out of the corner of my eye.

Jack stood regally next to the surfboard and faced the group, like a king addressing his subjects. He waved imperiously to David. "Thank you, David, and all my Mermaid teammates for such a warm welcome. I hope I can live up to the introduction. It's a real thrill to be part of this wonderful organization and an honor working alongside David."

Queenie made the international gag sign. "My God, if Jack shoves his nose into David's ass any farther, he won't be able to breathe."

No kidding. I've met some champion-ass kissers in my time, but Jack Tyne took sucking up to an art form.

Jack glanced around the room and quickly added. "And of course, all of you. I am humbled and sure I'm going to learn a lot from all of you. As David so accurately stated, GOOFYFOOT is an iconic surf brand and the foundation of the surf industry for fifty years." Jack caressed the fin of the surfboard like he would a lover's cheek. "This hand-cut longboard is one built by the founder of the company behind his parent's beach house on the north shore of Oahu, Hawaii'." Jack pointed to the ceiling. "While Paul Kamana went on to ride the big wave in the great beyond, the spirit of the surf lifestyle he helped create lives on in all of us who are fortunate enough to go GOOFYFOOT through life. To get you started, I've brought treats and GOOFYFOOT goody bags." Jack pointed to the goody bags on David's desk. "David, please pass out those bags to everyone?"

As though he worked for Jack and not the reverse, in his haste to do Mr. GOOFYFOOT'S bidding, David nearly collided with Jack. Holy guacamole. Amazing the boss had no idea how badly he embarrassed himself.

Jack enthusiastically clapped his hands as though addressing an excited group of kindergarteners on a field trip. "Ok, everybody, it's time to go GOOFYFOOT! Everyone put those leis around your necks, get those shades and logo caps on."

Queenie smirked. "And for his next trick, is he gonna lead us in the Hawaiian hokey pokey?"

Jack beamed a megawatt grin to the group. "I look forward to being a part of such a great team. Thank you again, David, for giving me this awesome opportunity." Jack tipped the bill of his cap to the executives and took his seat next to David.

David's eyes sought mine, and mistaking the message sent in his glare proved impossible. "*This is why I'm the boss, and you're not.*"

Maybe Jack Tyne would work out fine. I hoped so, for all of our sakes. And if not, I'd done my best to warn David. Jack Tyne was his problem, not mine. As if. I bit my lip to quash the laugh dancing on the tip of my tongue.

****

Queenie and I rarely had time to go out for lunch anymore. But only days after Jack's introduction, an emergency of epic proportions arose, and we needed to talk someplace off-campus and regroup.

Queenie gulped a fortifying swig of iced tea and groused. "My phone hasn't stopped ringing for two days. Every one of my reps called screaming their bloody heads off. Surfer Jack cut their territories and made their biggest customers into house accounts. He's reduced commission rates, cut their draws against commissions, and now reps are responsible for one hundred percent of their market week expenses." Queenie drummed her fingers on the edge of the table. "I've got a full-scale rep revolt on my hands, and I'm helpless to stop it."

I widened my eyes. "No kidding. I got the same calls. Since I ran the division before Jack replaced me, all the reps assume I have some say in the matter. As if. David is gaga for Jack, and I'm still in the doghouse." My laugh came out bitter as burnt coffee. "I'm the *last* person on Earth able to help the reps."

Queenie held out her hands. "I told them I have no control over anything Jack does, and to call David about their complaints. A dozen calls later, I stopped answering the phone."

I waved my cell phone in the air. "I took mine off the hook."

Queenie ran her fingers through her hair. "This *must* stop. We'll never get any work done."

I gave her a helpless look. "What could we do?"

Queenie bunched her shoulders. "To stop the madness, we need to tell David everything going on."

I put my palm straight out, like a traffic cop working Times Square at rush hour. "Hold on, sister. I wish I'd

17

listened to you, kept my trap shut, and never given David the lowdown on Jack. I'm sorry Jack stuck it to the reps, but I'm not willing to lose my job defending them. They're all adults. Let them fight their own battles."

Queenie made a sour face. "I'm not saying we tell David to reverse Jack's new deals. We just describe the crazy calls we're getting. Ask his advice on handling the situation. David's no dummy, and he's always been pro sales rep. He needs to hear everything Jack's doing and draw his own conclusions."

I sighed. "I'll go, but you're doing all the talking. If I get fired because of this, I will make sure you come with me."

****

Queenie squared her shoulders and faced the boss. "David, we're getting inundated by calls from reps regarding changes Jack implemented in their sales agreements." She smiled an engaging smile and dipped her head. "Because of the unilateral changes Jack's made, the reps are all ready to bolt. Any suggestions on handling this mess?"

I stupidly piped in my two cents. "Are you *aware* of the changes Jack made?" Good grief. I must have a death wish.

David glared at the two of us, but he directed the lion's share of his ire at me. He snapped as nastily as a cranky turtle. "Of course, I am. And frankly, you two ought to take a few lessons from Jack in management techniques. We finally hired a division president working on behalf of the company." David's voice dripped sarcasm. "The organization paying *your* salaries instead of coddling a bunch of whiny reps. They've bellyached to me as well, and I'll tell you the same thing

I told them. Jack is doing the right thing by making reps more responsible for company profitability. If the reps aren't happy, let them quit." Peevish David pointed to Queenie. "You ought to make the same changes in your division. Several low-profit margin groups of yours could stand some improvement."

Only a fool lectures Queenie Levine. She mounted her high horse, ready to ride roughshod over David and take us both straight to the unemployment line. "Since when did reps and management morph into an adversarial relationship at our company? As Jack told the salesmen, he runs his business his way, and I run my business mine. I hope we stave off every rep resigning." Queenie narrowed her eyes. "Want my take on the situation? This whole list of changes is calculated to get all our reps to quit his division and allows Jack to bring in his own sales force. Jack's shenanigans are bad enough, but you applauding him instead of stopping him is the most disturbing."

Holy guacamole. What kind of quicksand had I stepped into? The kind with my career sinking in it before my eyes.

Chapter Four

I cupped my ear. "Come again. He did *what*?"

Talented juniors swimwear designer Lynnie Stubbs sniffled as she swiped at the tears dribbling her cheeks. "Jack fired me. He barely glanced at my sketches and said we weren't a good fit for one another." In her early twenties, dark-haired, flat-chested Lynnie honked into a sodden tissue, giving a great imitation of a wounded goose. "How could he come to that conclusion if we never worked together?"

I clucked my tongue. "Such a crock. Your big problem is you've got a mind of your own."

Lynnie's fashion-forward designs were the reasons for the juniors division's success and the huge corporate expansion of the category. Lynnie deserved a promotion, not a kick in the ass. Everything she accomplished, she'd done all on her own. She'd juggled three menial jobs to supplement her scholarship to get through design school. Lynnie was a kind, decent young woman who served meals to the homeless on Christmas and volunteered weekends at an animal shelter.

The sound of fear shook in her tinny voice. "What am I gonna do now? There are no swimwear companies with any design openings this time of year. I live from paycheck to paycheck as it is. I can't be unemployed for a day, let alone a whole season."

Unfortunately, she was right. Every swimwear

line's design staff was already in place for this season. Vendors wait to make designer changes for the next season until after the current collections hit the stores. I wrung my hands in frustration. "I can't undo it. But I can try to keep you on board by doing something for me. Go back to your office and chill out. I'm going in to see David."

As I turned down the hall to David's office, I fought an internal battle. David and I were still on shaky ground. The last thing I wanted to do was to add to Lynnie's troubles. It would be my fault if I confronted David, and he takes his anger at me out on Lynnie by letting her go with no severance or letter of recommendation. But s*omebody* needed to speak on her behalf, or she'd be out the door through no fault of her own. And if not me, who? No one. I put on my big girl panties and leaned into his open door. "David? Got a few minutes?"

He gave me an expectant look and waved me in. Not exactly a greeting like he would his long-lost auntie, but at least the door wasn't slammed in my face. I sat across from David, prepared to put my job on the line. Never one to beat around the bush, I minced no words. "Jack fired Lynnie." He said nothing, but David's eyes widened enough to fill the lenses of his glasses. I took it as a good sign and went on. "The guy barely glanced at any of her sketches but made a snap decision to let her go. Her designs blew out of the stores." I made a fist and smacked it against the edge of his desk. "The man is a moron. Her line is the reason the division is so successful. First, he dumps the sales force, now, he fires the designer. Can't you see something is wrong with this picture?"

David warned me off with the cold glare of his dark

eyes. "Don't go down that road. This is Jack's baby now, and he has to be comfortable with his team." David shrugged. "What do you expect me to do? I can't countermand all his decisions."

I scoffed. "Why not? You certainly have no problem doing it to the rest of us."

David's expression clouded along with my window of opportunity. It served no purpose to win the battle and lose the war. I held my hands up in surrender. "I'm not here to rag on you. I came to see if you'll let me keep Lynnie. There's no room in the private label budget for a designer, but I could use her in product development."

David clucked his tongue. "We're not running a charity for out-of-work designers."

I made no attempt to leave the pleading out of my tone. "Please, David. Let me do this."

David made a sour face and sighed. "All right. I'll let you keep her, but with a twenty-five percent pay cut."

I'd take a big risk pushing the envelope any further. But I needed to fight for Lynnie the way it counted the most: In her wallet. "Geez, such a big pay cut is gonna be tough. She's already the lowest-paid designer. Is that your final offer?"

David had the grace to look apologetic. "I'm sorry, but yes. Product development assistants don't warrant a designer's pay scale. It will be hard enough justifying her at all to Harvey and the board, so take it or leave it."

I accepted before he reneged on the offer. "I'll take it. I'm gonna go tell her now." Not exactly an apology, but it was David's way of signaling the end of the problem between us.

****

The pall of defeat dulling Lynnie's eyes broke my

heart. I'd pay good money to run Jack Tyne through a woodchipper, or at least out the door. I gave Lynnie my most reassuring smile, but no sugar coating. An embarrassing demotion meant a huge career step backward, but at least she still had a job. "I've got good news and bad news. The good news is David let me keep you as a product development assistant. The bad news is a twenty-five percent pay cut." I squeezed her arm. "I'm sorry, Lynnie. I tried my best, but at least you'll be making something while…"

A gigantic smile spread across her face as she launched herself at me and danced us around her office in a crazy quilt kind of polka.

****

Lynnie put a stack of test lab reports marked Maxmart on my desk. "Everything passed, so I'll send these to the buyer." She blushed and stared down at her shoelaces. "Believe me, I'm grateful for the job." Lynnie shuddered. "But if David doesn't take care of the rat infestation in the lab, I'm gonna quit. The dogs and I will be forced to move into my parents' house until I find something else, but I won't work in a place with rats. My grandparents live in Manhattan Beach." Lynnie wrinkled her nose as though she had taken a whiff of yesterday's garbage. "Rats have been a problem for as long as they've lived there. My gramps uses some strong stuff on his own to control the rats between the exterminator's monthly visits. I'll get the name of the stuff Gramps uses and bring some to work."

I waved off her solution to the rat problem. "Relax. David's on it. He's heard complaints about the rats from half the staff. The exterminators will be in the building all weekend. The pest control company doing the job is owned by Earl Bernard. He's the chairman of our board of directors and our biggest investor. The building will be rat-free by the time we open on Monday. The dampness of that part of the building attracts the rats like it does at the beach. Queenie's two cats take care of her rodent issue. I'm deathly allergic to cats, but a lot of them roam around my marina. They must take care of the rats as I've never seen any, not even under the gangplank or near the garbage bins. Your grandparents should get a cat."

Lynnie shook her head no. "Not an option. My gram is also allergic to cats. Hopefully, this exterminator will take care of the problem." Lynnie smiled a Mona Lisa smile.

I cocked a brow. "Why the weird smile?"

Lynnie dipped a shoulder. "Carrie Le Beau paid me a visit earlier this morning."

I spun the mental Rolodex. Carrie Le Beau, Carrie Le Beau... Familiar name. But no luck placing it. "Who?"

Lynnie pursed her lips. "The new juniors designer."

Ah, yes. I remember her now. When Jack Tyne arrived at Clothing Concepts, Carrie Le Beau was the assistant swimwear designer. After head designer Louis Chennault's murder, the smart money said the up-and-coming assistant gets the top job. But that's not what happened. Instead, sexy Carrie became Jack's design assistant for the juniors division. Determined to move up, conniving Carrie, only a few years the senior of Jack's high school-aged son, viewed the boss as her best ticket into the big leagues. The industry gossip said Carrie earned the promotion to Mermaid's juniors division head designer job by working on her back.

Lynnie held out the fabric swatches. "I sat at my desk cutting the swatches. When I looked up to grab a hard stock card to mount the swatches on, I see Carrie standing at the entrance to my office. I wanted to slam the door in her face, but I'd been raised better. So, I invited her in."

I asked, "What did she want?"

Lynnie frowned. "She said somebody in the lunchroom mentioned my name. She came to see if they were talking about me."

I scoffed. "Why? Is there another Lynnie Stubbs working at Mermaid?"

Lynnie crossed her eyes. "No, of course not. Carrie and I went to design school together, and I called myself Lynetta back in the day." Bitterness tinged Lynnie's sad laugh. "Yeah. I dreamed of becoming some world-famous designer, and Lynetta sounded more sophisticated." Lynnie smiled. "Half the time I wouldn't respond if someone called me Lynetta, so I stopped using it." She glanced at the fabric swatches and sighed. "Besides, Lynnie suits me more. I asked if she needed something or was she here to…." Lynnie blushed from her neck to her scalp. "I debated whether to say gloat, but I took the high road and said, chat."

I gave her the big eyes. "So, which one was it?"

Lynnie scuffed the carpet with the toe of her tennis shoe. "She said she came to say hi and we should do lunch once things aren't so crazy. She sees the stack of pattern cards on my desk and asks the place to find them. I wanted to be snarky and say check in the lunchroom. But I played nice in the sandbox and told her to see Bernice in patternmaking. She asked if she could snag any extras, so I spotted her a dozen from my emergency stash I keep in the back of my storage closet."

I folded my arms across my chest. "So, what did Carrie *really* want?"

A rare flash of anger sparked from Lynnie's kind eyes. "To mark her territory and put me in my place."

I turned my head to see who it was when Jack Tyne walked past my open door holding a *West Coast Apparel News* under his arm.

I made a sour face. "Jack and David *do coffee* together every morning. Yesterday I walked into David's office to ask a question in the middle of their coffee klatch. From David's glare, you'd think I interrupted him while he made love to his wife. They're sipping and laughing like a couple of Yentas, but David said I'd intruded on a meeting and told me to come back later. Even though David's is an open-door policy, he said next time to knock."

Lynnie pointed to Jack's disappearing backside and laughed. "And you can set your watch by him. An hour later, Jack downs another coffee in his office, then heads for the men's room."

Chapter Five

Mystical Dreamer Swimwear National Sales Manager Sonia Wilson turned to me during one of our Yenta morning coffee klatches. "So, things still going ok now, considering all the changes at Mermaid?"

I asked, "I assume you're referring to Jack Tyne?"

Independent sales rep Joan Binder indelicately snorted. "Well, she doesn't mean Jack and the Beanstalk."

I gave Joan the stink eye. "Smartass. You worked for David for a long time. What's your take on things?"

Joan's startling violet eyes sparkled mischievously. "Let me guess. David didn't do any vetting, brought Jack in, and gave him carte blanche. Now it's not going according to David's plan, and he's looking for someone to blame."

Leave it to clever Joan to figure it out. "Yep. In a nutshell, you hit the highlights." Heads nodded as I surveyed the table. "If you remember, David gave me quite a tongue-lashing to mind my beeswax when it came to Jack's business practices. So, the boss caught me completely off-guard by his asking me to sit in on Jack's line reviews. Apparently, David hadn't brought Jack up to speed on his concerns."

Ditzy Swimwear showroom manager Hope Greenberg asked, "Why do you say so?"

I grinned from ear to ear. "Mr. GOOFYFOOT

turned green as grass when I sashayed into the design studio and plopped my tush between David and our head designer, Gary Burkett."

Sonia widened her eyes. "So, is the product hot? I bet it is. Carrie Le Beau is a first-rate juniors swimwear designer."

I dipped my head. "Halfway through the GOOFYFOOT presentation, David yawned and Gary checked his watch twice. A quarter of the way through the fashion line presentation, I whispered to Gary. "There's nothing new in the Sizzle collection. Jack only recolored last year's prints." Gary whispered back, "So far, your retreads are the best thing I've seen."

Sonia's jaw dropped. "Are you sure *Carrie Le Beau* designed the lines? She's a top-notch designer. She won several awards at design school. My old boss at Itsy Bitsy tried to steal her from Clothing Concepts. He offered her a bucket of bucks and a generous package of bennies, but she had no interest in moving from CC to a small company."

Hope raised her brows. "If she's so good, how come the product turned out so crappy?"

I dipped my head. "Lynnie and Carrie lunched after the line review. Carrie made it sound as though Jack wouldn't let her design the lines the way she wanted to. She implied Jack instructed her to only design the surf line and drop Sizzle completely. Carrie said she convinced him to at least let her recolor last year's Sizzle prints."

Hope asked, "And the surf line? No better? Surf is supposedly Jack's forte, right?"

Sonia shook her head slowly in amazement. "No better? Honest?"

"You'd think so, since he claims surf is his thing." I held up my fingers in the Girl Scouts honor hand signal. "But nope. It was far worse, if you ask me."

Sonia's eyes bugged. "Why?"

I said, "The surf prints weren't from our usual print houses. They came from the GOOFYFOOT print library. I guess Jack wanted the vintage look, but he forgot who the customer is." I laughed. "Bowling balls are more feminine than their patterns. Even recolored in girlie colors, the prints are dead ringers for my dad's aloha shirts."

Joan tapped her lower lip. "David's level of experience in the juniors market is less than the missy, but his styling eye is first-rate. I bet he wanted to kill Jack."

My smile bordered on evil. "Oh yeah. David had blood in his eye. He brought the models out after Jack completed the presentations. He said they are the consumer whose opinion counts and not ours, so, let's ask them their opinion of the product."

Sonia asked, "What did they say?"

I raised my brows. "The models were reluctant to say anything at first, but when David insisted, they took the gloves off and ripped those lines to shreds. Hated the dark colors and made fun of the dorky surf prints. One of them even recognized last year's recolored Sizzle prints. David offered all three a free bikini, and not one of them took a suit."

Joan's eyeglasses slid to the tip of her nose. "And Jack's reaction to this catastrophe?"

I deadpanned. "Jack said three giggly girls don't speak for the entire swimwear industry."

Mermaid division President Queenie Levine

shuddered. "I can only imagine David's response."

I pointed to a spot between my eyebrows and my hairline. "The blue vein in the middle of David's forehead danced the macarena."

Joan sucked in her cheeks. "What happened next? David's usual scream fest tantrum?"

I bit my lip. "No. Considering his hair-trigger temper, David was unnervingly dead calm. David told Jack the product must be revised, and to get Gary and Lynnie involved in the design and me in the merchandising."

Sonia said, "And Jack's response?"

I clucked my tongue. "Jack glared at Gary and me and said, 'Those three wouldn't recognize a great surf style even if it bit them in the ass.' "

Joan laughed and slapped the edge of the table. "Apparently, the same can be said for Jack."

Sonia pointed to her day planner. "So, are you guys working on it now? Starting from scratch this close to breaking a line is a heck of a challenge, but if you're focused and know what you're doing, it can be done. Even if there's not enough time to turn samples around, you can use fabric swatches and CADS for the first market, and the buyers will understand."

I rolled my eyes. "Nope. We're not doing anything."

Hope tsked. "What are you waiting for? Next season?"

I shrugged. "Not our call. Jack said he didn't need anyone's help, and he stood behind the product as it is designed, period."

Joan asked, "So, David fired him?"

I widened my eyes. "Remarkably, no. David said in life, everyone gets a rope, and either you save yourself or hang yourself by it. David gave Jack his rope and said he'd either live or die by it." I surveyed the table. "Maybe every dog does get its day. Even one as pedigreed and pampered as Jack Tyne."

My words turned out to be more prophetic than ever imaginable.

Chapter Six

After the server at Coast Pizza Parlor delivered our drinks Monday night, Queenie said, "Too bad you were out of town Friday. You missed all the fireworks."

I gave her a come again with the eyes and parroted. "Fireworks?"

Imitating a boxer, she clenched her fists and punched the air. "David and Harvey came close to blows."

David Workman is the undisputed king of the castle, but Chief Financial Officer Harvey Mazer is the keeper of the castle keys. Short, balding, cautious Harvey Mazer earned an MBA from Harvard Business School and is the one person at Mermaid who dared tell David Workman no and lived to see another day. David and Harvey rarely agreed on anything. Conservative bean counters such as Harvey drove risktaker David berserk.

Queenie said, "As I left David's office, Harvey barreled in, angry enough to bust a gut. Harvey left David's door open, so, nosy parker me, I stood out in the hall and listened in to their—" Queenie made quote marks in the air. "Let's be kind, and call it a *conversation*."

I scoffed. "No big deal. Their fights are a daily occurrence."

Queenie nodded. "True, but this time they almost got into a fistfight because of Jack Tyne. Harvey said,

'I've just spent a delightful twenty minutes getting an earful from Earl Bernard.' David snorted. 'So why are old Earl's boxers in a bunch this time? The cheapskate probably received an invoice for the swim dresses his wife ordered and wants a discount.' Harvey said, 'You wish.' Earl read our quarterly financial statement and went ballistic at our big fat loss. He was completely nuts at the costs for Jack Tyne's division. The separate sales force, separate design studio, separate designer, separate patternmaker, extra sample sewers, special trade show booth, separate New York showroom, and Jack's unsold one hundred thousand yards of fabric *wiped out the profits* from *all the other divisions combined.* But the costs of the GOOFYFOOT New York launch party that hardly any buyers attended made the old guy hyperventilate." Queenie choked on her scotch. "A real fun night."

I shivered at the memory. "An absolute blast if a root canal is your idea of a good time. Jack threw an expensive launch party, and no one came."

Queenie slapped the table. "Remember the photographer from the *Women's Apparel Journal* walking around the showroom, searching for an angle not focused on the emptiness of the place? With only six buyers on the huge dance floor, it was so empty, it looked like Madison Square Garden. We had enough leftover food to feed everyone lunch for the rest of the market week. If any other division president pulled such a stunt, they'd be fired on the spot."

I sighed. "Yet despite everything, Jack Tyne is still employed at Mermaid."

Queenie rested her index finger on the tip of her nose. "Jack Tyne appears out of the clear blue sky, is handed a proven, successful division on a silver platter, and David Workman gives the guy complete free rein to run the business as he wants. So far, the guy is a disaster, and yet, he still has his job. It makes you wonder if Jack's holding something huge over David's head?"

Perhaps the bartender put too much scotch in her drink? "What could Jack possibly hold over David?"

Drama Queen Ms. Levine batted her eyes. "Compromising pictures of David and another man."

I gave her the stink eye. "Aren't those David's wife and daughter in the photo on his desk?"

Queenie nodded. "David has a family, but the rumors in the market about him are persistent. Some years ago, during David's time as a swimwear buyer at Maritz Brothers, a story floated around the industry of him and Peter from Beachy Beach having a *special relationship*. The senior management at Maritz Brothers was on the conservative side. They passed over David several times for a management position he earned. The rumors stalled David's retail career and ultimately, drove him to our side of the business. Say the rumors are true, and Jack is blackmailing him?"

I shrugged. "A question we'd be hard-pressed to ever get the answer to." I gave her the big eyes. "And David's reaction to Earl's freak-out?"

Queenie rolled her eyes. "Typical David. He said ya gotta break a few eggs to make an omelet."

Holy guacamole. Chairman Earl Bernard is the richest and most powerful member of the Mermaid board of directors. He had the money and juice to get David fired. Maybe the boss lost his mind? "You must be kidding."

Queenie crossed her fingers on her heart. "Nope.

I'm not. Harvey said, 'I'd cut the cavalier attitude. I tap-danced some fancy footwork and managed to head off Earl and the board this time before they showed up here today. I doubt I'll be able to put them off again.' "

I slapped my cheek. "Good grief. What did they want?"

Queenie giggled like a naughty schoolgirl. "David asked the same thing. Harvey said right now, they want David's head on a platter. Jack's division has yet to write a single order, but the costs are astronomic. Earl flipped out comparing Jack's figures to yours last year at the same time. The board wants Jack out yesterday and threatened to bring in a minder for David in the form of a Chief Operating Officer to make sure David gives Jack the boot. Harvey said the board blames him for allowing David to bring Jack to Mermaid in the first place. The new person will be in charge of operations, and David and Harvey will both report to him. Earl gave David and Harvey two weeks to fire Jack and his team. If they don't recoup those lost profits in sixty days, he'd fire them both and make sure they never worked another day in the industry."

I turned to hand the server my water glass to refill as Jack and Carrie strolled in with their arms wrapped around one another. The hostess seated them at a booth diagonally across from us. "Speak of the devil." I angled my head at their table. "Guess who just got seated across from us?" I wrinkled my brow. "Weird. Carrie told Lynnie after the line review, she was super pissed with Jack."

Queenie followed my line of sight and smirked. "It appears they've worked things out."

I wiggled my brows. "Seems the rumors must be

true. Carrie earned the Mermaid gig working on her back."

Instead of answering, Queenie's eyes bugged as she pointed to a rather dowdy woman at the take-out counter. "OMG! See the fortyish, kinda plump, bleached-blonde at the take-out counter?"

My eyes followed her index finger. "Yeah. Who is she?"

Queenie shook her head slowly. "I barely recognized her. She's gained half a person and dyed her hair platinum, but the face is the same. It's Maureen MacDonald."

The name rang no bells. "And she is who?"

Queenie's voice took on a touch of reverence. "When I started in the biz, Maureen held the title of chief textile engineer at Gifford Mills, a southern-based fabric conglomerate with a rep as a good old boys' club. Apparel tongues wagged when Maureen's history-making promotion made her the sole female head textile engineer in the entire industry. A dozen engineers worked for her. All but one of them men."

I arched a brow. "You considered becoming a textile engineer?"

Queenie almost spilled her scotch down her blouse. "Good God, no. I'd never get through the chemistry."

I dipped my head. "So, how did you meet Maureen?"

Queenie said, "I started my career out of fashion school at Beach Scene Swimwear. Before being allowed to present the line to a buyer, sales reps were required to complete a merchandising and design segment. My boss Milton asked Maureen to write a technical manual for salespeople. She came to the factory and explained the manual to all the reps. A year later, out of the blue, she met a guy, got married, and left the industry." Queenie slapped her forehead. "OMG! I'm such a dolt. I should have put it together. The guy she married? Must be Jack, the juniors swimwear salesman at Beach Scene. I bet Milton introduced them. If I remember right, Jack founded a nonprofit charity getting inner-city kids into surfing. He convinced the entire juniors swimwear industry to get involved. The charity funded the surfboards, the wetsuits, the rash guards, swimwear, and other apparel, and even provided buses to and from the beach as well as supervised training. Beach Scene sponsored the charity with Jack, its company representative. Gifford also sponsored the charity, and Maureen represented them."

I said, "It still exists. Both Ditzy and Sizzle are Urban Surf Charities corporate sponsors."

I ping-ponged my eyes between Maureen and Jack. "Are you going down that road?"

Queenie smiled tightly. "You betcha. Jack Tyne. Beach Scene is a huge company. With me in the missy area and him in juniors, and the divisions in different buildings with separate management, it's not surprising we never crossed paths. But I should have recognized his name. Holy cow. Maureen married Jack Tyne." A weird expression crossed Queenie's face. "Jack is certainly consistent in his choices of women." Queenie drew an imaginary line from Maureen to Carrie. "You see Carrie Le Beau? Blonde, blue-eyed, stacked, and built à la Mae West? Back in the day? That's smoking hot sexy Mo Mac to a T."

Queenie turned her head to the sound of her name and found Mo Mac standing at our table. Mo Mac air-kissed Queenie and squealed. "Queenie Levine!" She gave Queenie the once-over and patted her cheeks. "Good gravy, girl. You haven't changed a bit." Mo Mac self-consciously tugged on the edge of her oversized, ratty sweatshirt and laughed. "Betcha can't say the same for me. How the heck are ya? Still party hearty?"

Queenie smiled. "Nah, not so much anymore. Guess I outgrew it. You?"

Mo Mac dipped her head. "No. Me neither. Marriage and kids tend to cramp your party style."

Queenie asked, "Still live on the silver strand?"

Mo Mac wiggled her brows. "Sure do. I got married, and when the kids arrived, we bought the biggest lot on the Silver Strand and built a humongous house. And you?"

Queenie held out her ringless left finger. "I'm still waiting for Prince Charming's arrival. I've got two pampered pussycat roommates. We're in a townhouse off Sand Dune on Quarterdeck east of Speedway."

Maureen fondly cuffed Queenie's arm. "Good gravy! We are so close, we could throw rocks at each other. Are you still in swimwear?"

Queenie swept an arm to me. "Gee, I'm so sorry. Where are my manners? Mo, this is my friend and colleague Holly Schlivnik. We're both at Mermaid Swimwear. I'm president of the missy division, and Holly is president of private label."

The color drained out of Mo Mac's face. "Mermaid?" She spat the company name out like she would a chunk of wormy apple. "You work with my husband Jack? He's at the same company."

Queenie gave me the big eyes. From the restaurant entrance to our table, no way Mo Mac missed Jack and

Carrie necking like horny teenagers. Queenie feigned surprise. "Isn't it a small world? Of course, we do. Great guy. Glad he's on the team."

Mo Mac angled her head towards the takeout counter. "My pizzas should be ready. Our son played his first varsity basketball game tonight. Venice beat Palisades, one of their big rivals. We're having a little team celebration at our house." She checked her watch and laughed. "Better hustle my bustle before the natives get restless and clean out the refrigerator. I'll get your contact information from Jack, and we'll do lunch, ok?"

Mo Mac and Queenie exchanged the second round of air kisses. As Mo Mac turned to leave, she and Jack locked eyes as he kissed Carrie's neck. Jack grinned, took off his logo cap, and the arrogant jerk tipped it at Mo Mac.

I kept staring at Jack. Something seemed different, but I couldn't put my finger on it. I racked my brain. A moment later, it came to me. I mentally snapped my fingers. His hair. I jutted my chin in Jack's direction. "Is Jack losing his hair? But it's not the way most guys going bald look. It's as though someone randomly yanked clumps of hair out from his scalp. Think he's sick?"

Queenie tapped her lower lip. "Dunno. He doesn't act sick. He's kinda young for it to happen, but his baldness could be hereditary. Maybe his hair just grew weird?" Queenie's eyes followed Mo Mac's disappearing backside and laughed an evil laugh. "Or, maybe his wife is poisoning him."

Chapter Seven

I completed my ten-minute presentation, and David waved his glasses at Jack. "Ok, pal, you're next. Let's hear the status of juniors and kids. We're all anxious to be brought up to date with our latest and greatest divisions."

Jack proudly drew his shoulders back and gushed. "I'm happy to report all the reps received their samples, and so far, the salesmen are getting a fantastic reaction to the product. "

Jack stopped speaking, and one helluva pregnant pause sucked all the air out of the room.

Apparently, the guy needed some prodding. David raised his bushy eyebrows. "And?"

Jack threw his arms skyward. "And? And now you've been brought up to date with the juniors and kids division."

David fanned the table. "All the other division presidents gave a rather detailed accounting of the status of their businesses, and we expect the same from you. The purpose of these team meetings is to share everything going on in our businesses." David scoured a page in a computer report. "You received in a ton of production fabric, but nothing's been cut. Why not?"

Jack shrugged. "Ike and I worked, but he wanted to wait."

David's glare could have melted an iceberg. "Wait

until when? The end of the season?" David flipped a few more pages of the report. He tapped the page with a pen. "Well, here's why. None of your orders are in the system. No wonder Ike wanted to wait. How would he know which styles or the number of units per color to cut? If you're having problems getting customer service to process your orders, tell Kathy."

Jack's face turned the shade of day-old oatmeal. He stammered his explanation as nervously as a schoolboy caught cheating on an exam. "I-I h-have uh, a no- o- orders y-yet." He flashed a hopeful smile. "But the reps all say the reaction to the line has been fabulous. I'm sure the orders will be flooding in any day now."

The rest of us knew what was coming and sunk down in our seats. We were all glad we weren't Jack Tyne.

David snarled. "Your line's been out for weeks, and you have *no orders*? There's enough of your fabric clogging the warehouse to dress the entire country! I told you to reduce those fabric orders, but did you listen?" David's spot-on imitation of Jack hit a bullseye. "You're an expert in your field, and the rest of us are a bunch of clueless morons." David smacked the conference table with the computer report. "Listen, mister, we've spent a bucket of bucks on you and your cockamamie ideas of an exclusive showroom, separate sales force, and design team, and not a single unit sold yet for our trouble. You better have one helluva plan for fixing your problem."

Jack's reaction? An eerily serene smile. "David, I don't have a problem to fix. It's too early to be worried. We're fine. The reps only worked with small stores so far. Those stores never write early." Jack purred with the smugness of a well-fed cat. "Don't panic. It's all under control. We broke the lines at the New York market, and all the majors saw the product. So, no worries. Now you'll see the orders come pouring in."

David didn't buy a single word Jack peddled. "You had no reason to order *any* fabric, let alone the amount of yardage you placed. Since it is painfully clear you have no idea which styles to cut, do not cut anything, and I mean not a single unit unless I authorize it. "

Jack snorted his derision. "You're crazy. You better let me cut the units I want, or there won't be anything to ship. The reps will direct their stores on which styles to buy based on the ones we've cut."

Queenie and I pinched each other's arms so as not to laugh out loud.

David scoffed. "You call *that* a production plan? If it is, it's the most preposterous bunch of crap ever proposed. With no orders, there's no way to decipher which styles are the right ones to cut. We're not gonna use a crystal ball. Get some orders to base your projections on, and we've got something to discuss." David glared at Jack. "I suggest you get off your ass, get on the phone, get on a plane, and do whatever it takes to make it happen, or else."

****

A few days before the next management meeting, David bellowed over the intercom. "Queenie, Holly! 211!" We no sooner walked into his office, and David flipped open the computer report to Jack's division. "So, Whaddya two make of this?"

I glanced over her shoulder as Queenie ran a finger down the third column labeled Order Status. "Every order in Jack's division is unconfirmed."

David turned to me with an expectant eye. Ok,

buddy. You asked for it. But remember, when you ask me a question, you better be prepared for my answer. "My take is *someone* put a bunch of fake orders into the system." David turned white as a ghost. I finger circled a row of styles. "Any of these styles been cut?"

David's stricken face went ashen as he flipped the page to the cut and sold. "Unfortunately, everything. Every single unit of those styles on the report is all cut, sewn, and hanging in the warehouse."

My eyes bugged as I followed David's finger across the page.

Fear quavered David's voice. "And if your evaluation is right, I've only got myself to blame for this disaster."

Queenie gave me the big eyes. No kidding. Was the boss *actually* taking responsibility for something? Alert the media.

David gulped. "It's not unusual for unconfirmed orders to be entered into the system, so I authorized Ike to cut every single unit without a second thought."

Queenie stabbed the cap of her pen on the total at the bottom of the page. "There's enough finished inventory to outfit a small country. So, what does your Rockstar say for himself?"

David rolled his eyes. "Oh, he's got an answer for everything, except none of his make any sense. His goods are slated to ship at the end of the month." David pointed to the calendar on his desk. "We only have three days left to get the confirmations, or the orders won't ship on time. The charge-backs for late delivery will wipe out most of our profit. I gave him till today to get the orders confirmed. He swore we'd get the confirmations, but we're still waiting for them."

Queenie's eyes seared David with a glare hot as a blowtorch. "So, I'm confused." She pointed to me. "*We've* been summoned to the inner sanctum for what reason…?"

David had the grace to blush. "To call the buyers and ask them if they really gave Jack those orders."

Queenie squealed like a stuck pig. "Have you lost your mind?"

David jutted his chin. "Someone must be accountable for those goods."

Queenie snapped, "It certainly isn't *us*. Why not try the guy responsible for the division? You don't trust him?" Queenie snapped her fingers. "No problem. Get your superstar to make the calls in front of you. Put them on speakerphone to make sure your wonder boy is not talking to dead air." Queenie flourished an abracadabra problem solved with her hands and grinned.

David's shoulders slumped. "Honestly, I doubt he's ever met any of them."

For once, I kept my trap shut, but silently, I agreed. David's situation grew more precarious by the minute. If those orders fail to ship on time, Mermaid is in a heap of financial trouble. I'd bet the farm the day after they miss the delivery date, Earl Bernard boots David and Harvey out the door two steps after Jack. Desperate for answers, David appealed to our egos to get them. "You've both got strong relationships with those buyers. They'll tell you the truth. If anyone can get to the bottom of this, it's you two."

I bit my tongue not to laugh at the irony of his request. I looked him straight in the eye. "Don't shoot the messenger this time if the message isn't the one you want to hear. Remember, I *warned* you."

****

The next afternoon Jack appeared understandably confused as Queenie and I walked into David's office in the middle of their meeting. David spoke in a conciliatory tone, but Jack turned the same shade of gray as a gunboat. "Jack, since you're having such a tough time getting the order confirmations, I asked Holly and Queenie to help you out." David prompted us. "Ladies, please share your conversations with the buyers."

Queenie snapped her list open with a flourish. Jack squirmed in his seat, trapped like a burglar stuck in a chimney. "Maria at Purdines hasn't seen any junior vendors yet, nor given out any junior orders. Gina at Josie's Swim Heaven doesn't know who you are, nor has she been shown the line. Diane at Little Rose reviewed the line and passed. She said the silhouettes were salable, but she wasn't keen on the mannish surf line patterns, and the fashion prints were outdated compared to the rest of the market. She told your rep she'd take another peek if any new groups were added to the line."

Queenie finished, and I took my turn at bat. "Mandy at Ronnie's only wrote orders for existing suppliers and is waiting to see if there's any money left for new vendors. Pat McPherson is not adding any new vendors right now and told your rep to contact him after the first of the year. Jamie at Contemporary Casuals told your rep she'd decide if she'd write once she reviewed three other new vendors' lines."

Some days it's not so good to be king.

Chapter Eight

Every morning before the crack of dawn, I don sweats and sneakers, and Siggie and I walk two laps around the three-building apartment complex bisecting the Porto Paloma Marina. After the two laps, we take Palawan across Admiralty to Washington Street, going west until it dead-ends at the pier. Before the asphalt becomes sand, I stop at A Jolt of Java and get two biggie-sized to-go cups of high voltage blend coffees. One for me and one for Pop, the old guy I've befriended who fished from the same spot on the pier every day for a decade.

The old man sat in a frayed mesh and rusted aluminum beach chair hunched over the wooden railing, casting and recasting his line. Pop scratched behind Siggie's ears and mouthed his thanks as I handed the old man the coffee. I leaned over Pop's shoulder to check his catch. "Good morning, Pop. Are they biting today?"

The old guy glanced into the dented plastic bucket and laughed. "What should I do with them? Throw them back or use them for bait? Once you cut off the heads and tails and gut them, not much left for a fella to eat."

The old man glanced at the overcast sky and shivered farther into his thin windbreaker. As he took a restorative gulp of java, a strong yank on the rod almost pulled Pop out of the chair. Siggie barked when Pop cursed out loud as the old guy spilled hot coffee on the front of his T-shirt. The rod practically bent in half as Pop set the coffee cup under the chair and used both hands to regain control of the line. The old man's voice shook. "I hope whatever I caught doesn't snap the old rod in two. I'd hate having to replace it." Pop's false teeth clacked as he smiled at the memory. "I've fished with this rod since the time I wore short pants. They don't make 'em this sturdy anymore."

The old man gripped the fishing rod tightly in two gnarled hands. He leaned back in the chair and braced his feet against the wooden pier rail and prepared to do battle. The seasoned fisherman slowly let out some line to ease the pressure on both him and the fish. Pop pinched his squint and let out a groan from the strain of fighting the monster he'd hooked. He pulled in and released a few lengths of the nylon line several times. "The fish is getting tired." He laughed a gravelly laugh. "Good thing. I am too. I'm not as young as I used to be. As he reeled the catch in, the old man glanced at the plastic pail and snorted. "I'm gonna need a much bigger bucket."

Despite the cool onshore wind blowing in hard from the ocean, Pop used the sleeve of his windbreaker to swipe at the perspiration pouring from the old man's scalp line and drenching his face. Exertion colored his neck to the same shade as an eggplant.

As the old man cranked the spinner and slowly hauled the catch in, short, chubby, alabaster-skinned Andy sauntered across the pier. Andy stood next to Pop and mumbled good morning. Andy leaned over the pier railing to check the catching progress and yelled. "Holy mackerel! Old man, you've hooked you a surfer!"

Pop and I gave Andy a pitying you-must-be-crazy-

or-something glance. Pop summoned a burst of energy, hauled the rod over his left shoulder, and gave an enormous tug on the line. My eyes bugged as the battered, wet-suited body of Jack Tyne, still attached by his surf leash to his surfboard, flopped unceremoniously onto the pier. Pop, Andy, and I stared at one another. As long-time pier locals, we'd seen a lot of crazy things, but nothing compared to this. We inched closer to the crumpled body, hopelessly entangled in the fishing line for any sign of life. Andy cautiously toed his faded deck shoe against the left leg of the prone body. "Is the guy dead?"

Nearsighted, the old man squinted into the sun and shrugged. Pop bent closer for a better look. Siggie rested his head on Pop's arm as the old man studied Jack's pummeled face. "He reminds me a bit of the guy who surfs every morning. Gets to the beach at the same time as me."

Andy blinked his confusion. "Which guy?"

Pop said, "The middle-aged guy and the hot blonde stacked chick usually wrapped around him on the beach. You've seen them around. They're the ones making out like a couple of horny teenagers or taking photos of one another on their phones. Sometimes she stands next to me and takes pictures of the idiot daredevil surfers coming in through the pier pilings." Pop jerked his chin at Jack. "Another one of those hotshot morons."

Andy glanced at Jack's ravaged face. "No way to tell now. Besides, I never got close enough to see the guy. What about you?"

Pop said, "I mighta, but mebbe not." Pop took his cap off and scratched the crown of his head. "Hard to remember the brand of cereal I ate for breakfast most days, let alone some surfer and his groupie chick."

I pointed at Jack. "This guy works at the same company I do." Pop and Andy looked at me surprised, as though they'd forgotten I was standing right next to them. "And the woman you're describing is someone who works with us too. Did either of you guys see them this morning?"

Pop shook his head no.

Andy's double-chin quivered with the gyrations of a bowl of Jell-o as he jerked it towards the end of the pier. "Not him, but on my way to the pier, I passed a woman walking east on Washington who might be the chick Pop described."

Since Jack hadn't so much as twitched, Pop angled his leathery face closer to Jack's pasty grayish kisser to see if he was as dead as he looked. Pop leaned in and passed a hand over Jack's mouth.

Pop took a breath, and Siggie barked when the old man jumped back as though he'd been burned by a cattle prod. The sickening stench wafting out from Jack Tyne's wetsuit could easily fell an entire herd.

The old man gagged as his eyes followed a wavy line of caked yellowy vomit haloed around Jack's blue lips, chin, and the stub of a beard. Pop dragged his eyes past Jack's ravaged face to the watery streams of greenish-brown crap leaking out of the sleeves and legs of the torn wetsuit. Pop jumped a helluva lot faster than you'd expect a guy his age ought to as the liquidy turds slowly coursed onto the deck of the pier.

Andy playfully poked his elbow in the old man's ribs and joked. "Whatssamatta? The guy's breath that bad?"

The old man pointed a crooked index finger at

Jack's pummeled body. "Poor bastard doesn't have any breath at all. He's dead as a doornail."

Naturally, I burst out laughing.

Let me just say genetics aren't all they're cracked up to be. Lucky me. I inherited my nana's fear of death. We both overcompensated for it with the nervous habit of laughing.

Chapter Nine

Given the nosy nature of the human species, it came as no surprise that in no time flat, a dead guy attached to his surfboard laid out on the pier attracted a rather loud and boisterous crowd. Since none of the gawking looky-loos called the cops yet, I retrieved my cell phone from the back pocket of my sweatpants and dialed nine-one-one.

Ten minutes later, two blonde buffed Venice division surfer-wannabe cops wearing blue T-shirts stenciled LAPD in white across their chests, dark navy uniform shorts, and safety helmets arrived mounted on ten-speed bikes.

The crowds parted to let the Beach Boys in drag get to the location of all the excitement. They bent at their knees level to Jack's body, took a whiff, and the highly trained, experienced law enforcement professionals ran to the pier railing and lost their breakfasts. This might not be a case of another stupid surfer who'd accidentally drowned trying to ride the waves between the pier pilings. The taller cop grabbed the radio off his service belt and called it in.

LAPD detective Akira Jane "AJ" Yakamura arrived on the scene twelve minutes later. Average height and pencil-thin, the nearsighted, plain-as-vanilla-pudding cop was a gum-popping ex-smoker who surprised many with her potty mouth and sarcastic sense of humor. AJ and I go back a long time. She is married to Buster Schumansky, the LA sales rep I worked with during my stint at Ditzy Swimwear.

Siggie and I stood between Pop's aluminum chair and Jack's corpse. AJ said in a tone that said it was anything but, "This is a big surprise." Siggie woofed good morning when AJ squatted to scratch him behind the ears. The detective grinned. "If it isn't the grim reaper of the apparel mart right in the thick of it for a change."

I made a sour face. "Good morning to you too, Detective."

She waved a greeting to the uniforms and glanced at the corpse. "The vic familiar, or are you one of the looky-loos?"

I said, "He worked at our company."

AJ shook her head. "Why do I even bother asking?" She sighed with resignation. "You know the drill. I'll need a statement sometime today. I'll call you later to schedule it."

I tilted my head towards Pop and Andy. "Talk to the old man and the chubby guy standing next to him. The old man is the one who hauled Jack in, and Andy, the younger one, helped him. They mentioned recognizing Jack and a woman at the beach every day. From their description, she is someone who works at my company too."

AJ spoke briefly to Pop and Andy who had been separated by the uniforms. A pair of reading glasses rested on the wide bridge of her nose. She pulled a small worn notebook out of her pants pocket, scribbled a few notes, handed Pop and Andy her business card, set up appointments to take their statements, and dismissed the two men.

AJ took one look at the gnarly gunk flowing out of the wet suit and pulled a small jar of Vapor Rub out of her jacket pocket. She pushed a bony index finger full of mentholated goo into her nostrils. She shoved a pink block of bubble gum into her mouth and chomped with the fervor of a chipmunk. She blew a bubble the size of a fifty-cent piece.

She circled the body holding a dainty hand-embroidered handkerchief over the nostrils of her flat, broad nose. AJ blew a bubble the size of a paperweight and used her pointy front teeth to pop it. She slipped on a pair of thin latex gloves she pulled out from an inside jacket pocket. The detective carefully zipped open the top back of Jack's wet suit and noted the name written in waterproof ink on the tag below his neck.

She motioned to the uniforms who'd finished draping yellow crime scene tape around the body and instructed them to comb the beach for Jack's stuff. The two uniforms glanced at Jack and gave the detective a grin, grateful to get far away from the stink.

The uniforms passed the Los Angeles County Assistant Coroner as she loped onto the pier. Oh goody. The morning turned into a regular old home week. Five-foot-eleven Sophie Cutler, MD, is a skinny, blonde, blue-eyed brilliant but nerdy scientist, and my life-long friend. We met the first day of junior high school in Mr. Hepburn's biology class and soon became a scholastic tag team. The idea of cutting into a frog made me nauseous, and Sophie proved incapable of writing a decent paper if her life depended on it. So, we struck a win-win deal. I wrote her essays, and she dissected my frog. It's how Snip became her nickname. I gave her a two-fingered salute. "Good morning, Snip."

Snip bent in half to hug me.

After she straightened up, she tapped her wristwatch and grinned. "Playing hooky?" I shook my head no. She pointed to the closed surf shops on Washington Street. "Too early to be shopping the stores, isn't it?"

I rolled my eyes. "Not shopping. It's my exercise regimen. Siggie and I walk from our dock to the pier and back every morning."

Snip waved east towards the interstate. "And why aren't you breaking every traffic law on the books trying to get to work on time?"

I pointed to Pop. "Siggie and I stood right next to him when the old guy fished Jack Tyne out of the water."

The good doctor's hands flew to her cheeks. "Fast worker, aren't you? The victim's probably still warm, and you already know his name."

I clucked my tongue. "Of course, I do. He worked at my company."

She smirked. "Now, this comes as a shocker."

I sighed. Some days you're better off staying in bed.

She narrowed her eyes. "Why are you still hanging around?"

She better ditch the unleaded stuff and start drinking the high-test coffee.

I scowled. *Why do you think*? Someone who worked at my company is dead, and I'm curious what happened to him."

She smirked. "So, you're being your usual nosy self."

I crossed my eyes. "Funny. If you enjoy a lobotomy."

She laughed. "Try not to get into trouble this time. At the last fiasco, you came awful close to getting yourself killed. I'd hate to see you end up as one of my patients." Snip batted her eyes. "I suppose you laughed?"

No sense denying it. We'd been friends too long, and besides, my reputation preceded me. "You need to ask?"

Sophie looked at AJ, and they rolled their eyes. Cripes. My friends. Go figure.

AJ grimaced as she passed Snip her jar of goo. "Trust me, you're gonna need this."

Snip put her black bag on the pier and slipped on latex gloves. She shoved a finger full of glop into her snout and squatted on her haunches next to Jack. After completing a cursory examination, she whistled and blinked her bewilderment at the detective. "What the Sam Hill happened to this guy?"

Detective Yakamura deadpanned. "Gee, Sophie, aren't you supposed to tell me?"

Looking for an easy fix to set the time of death, Snip checked Jack's wrists for a dive watch. Jack had his strapped to his right wrist, but the face had a huge crack down the center, and the watch stopped. She took a rectal thermometer from her medical bag and stuck it between the cheeks of Jack's pasty-colored behind. She monitored the time, removed the thermometer, and wrote the information on a form fastened to a clipboard.

Snip squatted to be at the same level as the body. She opened Jack's eyes and noted out loud some of his blood vessels had burst. She tipped his head back and observed the blood caked around his nostrils. Snip opened Jack's mouth and ran her index finger around his gums and held up her blood-covered fingertip to AJ.

She carefully pulled the wetsuit open wider and rubbed her fingertips lightly on the black-and-blue-striped bruising on Jack's abdomen and backside. As she expertly examined Jack's body for signs of rigor, her fingers brushed against something poking out of the wetsuit. She removed and bagged a key fob attached to a ring velcroed inside the wetsuit to Jack's leg and handed it to AJ.

After completing her field examination, Sophie respectfully pulled the wetsuit back around Jack. She stood and faced AJ. "It's gonna be tough to give you an accurate TOD. Body temperature drops more slowly submerged in water. Rigor set in, so I'd say he's been dead two hours."

AJ shuddered. "Any idea on the cause of death? I've seen drowning victims before. But this guy is such a wreck, something else must have killed him."

Snip removed the latex gloves and closed her medical bag. "Until I get him on the table, nothing official. But the crap-filled wetsuit and all the vomit said something catastrophic happened to him and caused him to drown. There are several bruises and contusions on the body, but it's undetermined yet if they are pre- or post-mortem. His gums and nose both indicated signs of bleeding. His was a violent ending, but it's to be determined whether the bleeding is a result of this trauma, or his blood was thin." Sophie wrinkled her brow. "I noticed one odd thing. I pulled off his hood, and clumps of hair fell out into my hands."

AJ narrowed her eyes. "This significant?"

Sophie dipped her head. "Not prepared to speculate at this point. It may be important, or the guy's hair loss is genetically created. I'll have a more accurate idea after I run a full tox screen and stomach contents on him."

One of the uniforms stepped between the two

women and interrupted them. The taller, younger one tipped his head towards the beach. "Excuse me, detective. I'm sorry to bust in on your conversation, but we found the victim's stuff. I left Eddie guarding the victim's belongings, so no one disturbed them. If you'll follow me, we'll show you everything we found."

Sophie waved to the medical examiner's crew, signaling to bag the body for the trip to the morgue. She turned to AJ. "I'll call you as soon as there's something definitive." Sophie pointed towards the beach. "If you find anything, it'll need testing. Bag it, and we'll get it to the lab."

AJ gave her the ok sign. "I'm on it. Talk to you from back at the shop." She mouthed goodbye to me, turned about-face, and followed the uniform to the beach.

With the help of smoke and mirrors, Jack Tyne danced through life relatively unscathed. But today, Jack learned the bitter lesson it's a pay-me-now-or-pay-me-later world no one escapes. And eventually, we all pay for our sins. I'd soon learn Jack Tyne's sins cost him his life.

I left my boss a voicemail to report the reason for Jack's absence and added I'd be extremely late. Cripes. Who says exercise is healthy for you?

****

I filled the Yentas in on the details of Jack's demise later that morning.

When I finished telling the tale, Joan shook her head. "Another Clothing Concepts alum takes a dirt nap. If you're keeping score, there's already one murdered, this one's dead from an unknown cause, and a third one is in prison for life."

Sonia grinned. "Not exactly great for recruiting.

Their reputation is now the roach motel of swimwear suppliers. You go into the company vertical, but you never come out the same."

Hope shivered, "And you witnessed it?"

I shuddered at the memory of Jack's corpse fished out of the ocean big as an overgrown flounder. "Yep. Standing right next to Pop when the old man hauled Jack in still attached to his surfboard and dropped him onto the Washington Street pier."

Joan pointed to the *West Coast Apparel News* spread out on the table. "The article said the cause of death is suspicious and under investigation."

Hope fanned her fingers. "Suspicious? The word is he drowned."

I said, "Yes, he drowned. But my friend Snip says given the condition of the body, something catastrophic *caused* him to drown."

Queenie grinned. "David had a plan to get rid of Jack. Bet this isn't the plan he had in mind."

Hope patted her cheeks. "If Buster's wife is involved, somebody had one."

Chapter Ten

The bar in the Star Café at fisherman's village in Marina del Rey sported quite a crowd for a weeknight. Thirty minutes and two Chardonnays later, Snip and I sat across from one another in a cavernous booth big enough to accommodate the infield of a major league baseball team.

I wasted no time on frivolous news, weather, and sports. "So, any conclusions yet on Jack Tyne's cause of death?"

Snip said, "Mr. Tyne's lungs were filled with saltwater, so, officially, he drowned. But he had help."

My innards twisted around tight as a corkscrew. "Somebody held his head underwater kind of help?"

Snip flicked her wrist. "Not in so many words. Help in the sense that at the time of death, he had enough thallium in his system to fell a whale. Thallium poisoning ultimately killed him."

I gave her the big eyes. "Thallwhoium?"

Snip replied, "Thallium is thallous chloride."

I pinned Doctor Death with a clock-stopping scowl.

Snip grinned. "Thallium is a tasteless, odorless, soluble element. Used originally as rat poison and similar to warfarin, Thallium has medicinal usage for those patients with AFIB. It works the same as rat poison by thinning the blood. Ingesting over one gram of thallium negatively impacts the human body in a significant manner, and poisoning is the result."

I dipped my head. "If it's odorless and soluble, how do you know it was in his system?"

Snip said, "Symptoms of thallium poisoning are nausea, vomiting, diarrhea, convulsions, loss of reflexes, muscle atrophy, and hair loss." She grimaced. "Sorry. I realize this is not exactly dinner table talk. I observed vomit on his face and neck and some rather nasty watery crap inside the victim's wetsuit."

Certainly not table talk, but I asked the question. "I'm no doctor, but it sounds like a bad case of the Tijuana trots."

Snip nodded. "You're right. A plate of bad clams gives the same symptoms, but there was no indication in the initial tests on his stomach contents to suggest he'd ingested any bad food. We're running a full tox screen on him now as well as on the liquid found in a thermos he'd left on the beach. His hair gave me the idea of thallium poisoning. I took his wetsuit hood off, and clumps of his hair fell into my hands. Hair loss is a classic sign of thallium poisoning."

I widened my eyes. "Interesting."

Snip made a funny face. "Why?"

I ran my fingers through my hair. "Jack always wore a logo cap at the office, so I never noticed his hair. One night my friend Queenie and I met at Coast Pizza Parlor at the same time as Jack. He took off his cap, and I couldn't miss his hair loss. But his bald spots were unlike those of most men going bald." I made a circular motion around the bottom of my head. "When Gramps lost his hair, he had nothing on the top and only a fringe of hair around the bottom of the scalp. But Jack's hair? Like someone pulled tufts of it haphazardly out of his head. It didn't look normal." I laughed, "Queenie said maybe his wife poisoned him."

Doctor Death snapped to attention and narrowed her eyes. "Why?"

I said, "The hostess seated Jack and his designer in the booth across from us. They carried on like a couple of horny kids. Jack's wife walked into the restaurant and caught him in the act. Believe me, if looks killed, he'd be pushing up daisies."

Snip's eyes widened. "Does AJ know about this?"

I sputtered with the drip of a leaky faucet. "O-Oh. C-Come. O-On. Of course not. Queenie said it for a laugh."

Snip tapped a finger on her lower lip. "The spouse is always the first one suspected."

I rolled my eyes. "You watch too many cop TV programs."

Snip made a sour face and continued. "Mr. Tyne didn't suffer from AFIB. Mr. Tyne had a healthy heart. So, there was *no* medical reason for him to ingest thallium or *any* type of blood-thinning medication. Other than the catastrophic events leading to his drowning, Mr. Tyne was a healthy man. If the tox screen is positive for thallium poisoning, someone went to a lot of trouble to murder him. Thallium is so powerful and dangerous that it's been banned in this country for any use. So, someone either had it a while or put in a lot of effort to get it. The guy drowned, but he had help."

So much for the quiche I'd been hankering for all day. I've got to stop asking so many questions.

Chapter Eleven

An odd expression was plastered across Lynnie's kisser when she walked into my office the next afternoon. "You'll never guess who called this morning."

I was never a fan of twenty questions. I gave her the international sign of move it along. "Ok, I'll never guess. So, who?"

Lynnie smirked. "Carrie Le Beau."

My jaw dropped. Carrie made such a scene when David let her go, security had to be called to escort her out of the building. "Good grief! Of all people. Why in the world did she call you?"

Lynnie grinned from ear to ear. "Career advice."

I burst out laughing. "You're kidding."

Lynnie crossed her heart. "Nope, I swear."

I funneled my lips. "So, you offered her career advice?"

Lynnie sighed. "It's not that I wanted to. But she sounded so pathetic, I agreed to meet her for lunch." Lynnie grimaced and wrinkled her brow. "She's a walking disaster. If I passed her on the street, I wouldn't recognize her. Disheveled, grungy clothes like she hadn't changed outfits in a few days, and greasy, bedhead hair. Red and puffy eyes said she'd been crying, but oddly, she wasn't all too broken up over Jack's death."

Hard to fathom. A vision of Carrie and Jack wrapped around one another at the pizza joint buzzed inside my memory banks. "You sure?"

Lynnie nodded emphatically. *"Definitely.* She ragged on and on that Jack wouldn't let her design the lines the way she wanted, and his terrible styling directions got her fired. She said Jack destroyed her career and her great future at Clothing Concepts with his pie-in-the-sky promise of bigger things to come by going with him to Mermaid."

I scoffed. "No one held a gun to her head."

Lynnie scrunched her nose as though she'd sniffed yesterday's garbage. "Talk about uncomfortably awkward? It was a relief when we switched to news and weather, but I couldn't spend all day with her. I tried prompting her, so she'd get to the point, but she danced all around the reason she called me. She finally brought up jobs when the server brought the bill."

I shook my head sadly. "She must realize this time of year it's gonna be tough."

Lynnie wrung her hands. "Believe me, she does. Carrie's not one of my favorite people, but I'm no stranger to the squeezing in your gut when you're desperate for a job. I told her to use me as a reference, and I'd make a few calls. She received a month's severance, but even if she's thrifty, it's not gonna go far. While waiting for the server to bring me my change, we'd run out of the normal things to talk about. Out of desperation, our conversation turned to our grandparents. We compared notes and discovered both our grandfathers have medical issues. It turns out they are both difficult patients who never do as they are supposed to. My grandpa is diabetic, and my grandma constantly reminds him to test his blood sugar. Carrie said her grandpa has a heart condition. He says his medications make him feel weird. So, sometimes he pretends to take them, but he flushes the pills down the toilet instead. Carrie keeps some of his medication for an emergency if he runs short before the prescription is due for a refill."

Lynnie smiled. "I go to my grandparents every Sunday for dinner. Before I go home, my gram packs me a gigantic care package." She laughed. "I guess she thinks without it, I'd starve all week. She packs too much food for one person, and I end up freezing most of it. So, this Sunday, I stopped off at Carrie's on the way home and gave her the care package my gram packed for me."

I asked, "Does Carrie live near your grandparents?"

Lynnie shook her head no. "No, she lives in a cottage in Venice two blocks from the beach."

I mused. "She's been designing for a while, so I'm sure she's made decent money, but Venice is a trendy area. Some of those places, even the small ones, go for a million-plus. The monthly mortgage payment must be big enough to choke an elephant. How will she afford it? Since she's not working, will she be forced to sell it?"

Lynnie said, "There's no mortgage. Her grandfather owned the cottage free and clear since the 1980s. He signed the cottage over to her before he went into assisted living. It's one of those cool retro cottages painted in bright, funky colors. Hers is turquoise and white trim. It's tiny. One bedroom, one bath. It's cozy, but adorable. She furnished her living room with rattan and accented it with beachy antiques. The old-fashioned kitchen is minuscule. It was equipped with a two-burner gas stove and a small refrigerator with a pull-open freezer on top. We couldn't get all Gram's food into the dinky little space. We put most of it in the freezer section of the refrigerator in her garage."

I said, "She's lucky you're such a nice person. Anyone but you would tell her to go pound sand."

Lynnie's lips formed a secret Mona Lisa kind of smile. "What goes around comes around."

Lynnie Stubbs had no idea her words would turn out to be so profoundly prophetic.

Chapter Twelve

Queenie and I arrived at Jack's house around lunchtime to pay our respects. AJ's faded red sedan sat behind a minivan in Jack's driveway surrounded by three LAPD squad cars. There was no spot close by, so we parked around the block. Queenie's hand shook as she rang the doorbell. "With a fleet of police cars, either they're arresting Mo Mac, or she's barricaded herself in the house."

I pointed to the sedan. "Let's not get ahead of ourselves. AJ's car is in the driveway behind the minivan. Hopefully, she's not still angry at me for not telling her your comment about Mo Mac, and she'll fill me in."

Queenie rolled her eyes. "For crying out loud! Where's her sense of humor?"

I gave her the stink eye. "AJ said we should count our lucky stars we weren't run in for obstruction. So, I guess she missed the humor in your suggesting Jack's wife poisoned him."

Queenie said, "I called Mo Mac yesterday to make sure we could come today and pay our respects. She said David and Harvey sent a huge fruit basket from the company. Ike and Bernice sent a catered dinner from Beachside deli." Queenie asked, "Did Lynnie tell you she came here to see if Mo Mac needed any help?"

I shook my head no. "No, but Lynnie coming to see

Mo Mac isn't a surprise. Even though she had issues with Jack, Lynnie is one of those decent souls who rises to the occasion and does the right thing."

A uniformed LAPD patrolman with a buzz cut who looked too young to shave, let alone carry a gun, opened the front door.

Queenie said, "We're friends of Mrs. Tyne. Please tell her Queenie and Holly are here to pay our respects."

The kiddie cop apologized but held firm. "I'm sorry, but this is a police investigation. You'll have to come back another time."

He blinked his surprise when I said, "Tell Detective Yakamura Holly Schlivnik needs to see her."

He closed the door, and five minutes later, AJ opened it. She smiled a greeting, but backed up the kiddie cop. "The officer told you the correct information. You're not allowed inside."

I said, "I understand. Is Mrs. Tyne under arrest, or is she inside?"

"She's waiting in the backyard while we conduct our search." AJ sighed. "I shouldn't let you, but go on back." She pointed to her car. "Walk to the end of the driveway, and you'll see a gate to the yard on the right." She wagged her index finger under my nose. "Don't make me regret this."

I held out my hands. "We want to pay our respects, nothing more."

AJ rolled her eyes and closed the door in my face. Geesh. Friends. Go figure.

A kidney-shaped pool, jacuzzi, firepit, and built-in barbeque grill adjacent to wrought-iron patio furniture in the center completed the yard. We found Mo Mac sitting in an Adirondack next to an exotic-looking woman neither of us recognized. The woman held Mo Mac's hand and spoke to her softly, as if to a frightened, lost child. But Mo Mac just stared into the swimming pool as though the water held the answers to her problems. Past noon and Mo Mac was still in her bathrobe.

Mo Mac came back from never-never land and hugged us both fiercely. She patted the exotic woman's arm fondly and asked, "Do you know Mira Kumar? Mira and I went to textile engineering school together, and later she became one of my best engineers at Gifford." Mo Mac squeezed Mira's hand. "Now she owns Beach Rags, the hot beachwear line out of India."

I shook my head no. "No, we've never met."

Queenie smiled at Mira. "I've seen your line in the stores. It's so innovative. I love the fabrics you use."

Mira was dressed in an expensive designer tracksuit. Fortyish Mira's triangular face featured a smallish nose set between coal-black eyes and full lips. Wavy black hair pulled back in a low chignon laid against smooth skin the color of lightly toasted almonds. Average height, with a curvy figure and generous bust.

Mira spoke in a soft voice with the slight sing-song lilt of an Indian accent." It is nice to meet you. I am sorry it is under such terrible circumstances. I am humbled by your kind words." She pressed Queenie's hand between her two and laughed. "I took some fabric risks and am relieved the customers seem to accept the out-of-the-box concept. We have a showroom in the mart, but I am so involved in design and production, I rarely get there. So, I am not surprised our paths never crossed." Mira pointed to Queenie's sweater. "I love your sweater. I've never seen anything like it. The embellishments are exquisite. May I ask where you got it?"

Queenie was rail-thin. There was not an ounce of fat on her athletic body. It made no difference if it was winter or summer. Without much insolation, Queenie was always cold. She kept a sweater in her office and had it on most of the time. The sweater was a special one. She graduated with honors from Upton Fashion Institute, and the one-of-a-kind sweater she designed won a top award. The distinctive white ground, long-sleeved sweater was embellished with mother-of-pearl crafted into seashells of various sizes that covered the front of the sweater.

Queenie traced a finger across the cluster of shells on the front of the sweater. "Thank you so much. I made it. It was my senior project in fashion school." Queenie blushed from head to toe. "I won the top design award in my class with this sweater. A compliment from a first-rate designer like you means the world to me."

Mira leaned over and took a closer look at the sweater. "It's gorgeous. You're quite talented. You should consider going into the embellishment business. It's a hot category right now."

Queenie grinned. "Something to think about. If I do, maybe you could give me some design pointers."

We dragged a couple of wrought-iron patio chairs from a matching table closer to the two women. Once we'd settled in, Queenie turned her attention to Mo Mac. "It's bad, but are you holding up ok?"

Mo Mac barked a reply from deep in her throat that was someplace between a laugh and a cry. "Freaking dandy. It's been one helluva morning. You three are the first friendly faces I've seen. I got the kids off to school. Then the doorbell rings while I'm drinking coffee and reading the newspaper." She laughed a tinkly laugh like the sound water makes running over stones in a mountain creek. "The last time it happened, I remembered thinking it's kinda early for the Jehovah's Witnesses. Turned out to be the detective to tell me about Jack."

She pressed her lips into a thin line. "This morning, I open the door, and who do I find? Jack's latest whore coming to *pay her respects*. I slammed the door in her face, but she kept ringing the bell and yelling for me to let her in. Before every tongue on the block wagged, I opened the door and pulled her into the house." Mo Mac puckered her lips as though she'd bitten into a piece of rotten fruit. "The tramp gave me some cock and bull story that she no idea Jack had a wife or knew anything about the kids. Yada, yada, yada. She bursts into tears and tells me she's sorry for any pain she'd caused me and my children." Mo Mac's strangled laugh came out more like a sob. "Yeah, she actually thought I'd believe her stupid story."

"She asks to use the powder room to fix her face. She comes back, asks if we've set a funeral date and if I'd let her attend!" Mo Mac rolled her eyes. "I said, oh, sure, why the heck not, and asked if she wanted to sit in the family section too? The dumb broad took me seriously and thanked me for being so gracious. She couldn't understand why I threw her out of the house and told her not to come back."

Mo Mac pushed a clump of bedhead hair behind her ear. "An hour later, Detective Yakamura and a squadron of cops arrive. She shoved the search warrant in my face, and I said, give me the list of what you're looking for. I'll give you everything." Jack's widow spat. "I've nothing to hide. There was no need to do this. She refused to answer any of my questions. All she said was,

Mrs. Tyne, please step aside and let my team enter. The sooner my team and I start, the sooner we finish. I moved to the side, and three teams of two men came in carrying evidence bags and a ton of equipment. I followed her into the kitchen, but the detective stopped me. She told me to either sit in the living room or leave the house. So, I sat on the sofa and waited. Twenty minutes later, two patrolmen brought a huge bag out of the guest bathroom," She snorted. "And they were pretty pissed I dared to get in their faces. I asked for a list of the contents in the bag, and the baby-faced cop said no disrespect intended, but it's none of your business. He said if I interfered again, they'd make me leave until they completed the search." Mo Mac spoke through gritted teeth. "I said I should call my lawyer and find out if you're allowed to take anything. The kiddie cop told me to read the warrant. It gave them the authority to search the entire property and seize anything they deemed questionable."

I asked, "So, of course, you called your attorney, right?"

Mo Mac closed her eyes. I leaned forward to hear her when she whispered, "Ya want the truth? I've no idea if we even have a lawyer." She raked her fingers through her hair. "Crap, I drew a blank." She hung her head. "I caught myself before I finished dialing Jack's cell phone number to ask him." She squeezed Mira's hand. "A half-hour later, Mira arrived. The detective sent her to the backyard either to keep me company or to prevent me from drowning myself in the pool."

The disembodied voice of one of the uniformed policemen interrupted our conversation when he called out, "Detective, please come out to the garage. I found something you need to see."

Chapter Thirteen

I fought through the mob to get to the newsstand across from the mart deli. Gossipy tongues wagged at the screaming boldface headline above the fold in the *West Coast Apparel News*: *Swim Exec Murdered. Famed Textile Engineer Arrested.* I bought the last copy and headed for A Jolt of Java.

Queenie blanched, reading the headline. "Mo Mac is innocent, but even Rose Markowitz says it's bad."

Sonia laughed her throaty laugh. "You guys keep the old lady on speed dial?"

After being wrongly arrested for buying office executive Bunny Frank's murder, Sonia didn't have a lawyer. I called my uncle Barry, a personal injury attorney in Beverly Hills, for help, and he sang Ms. Markowitz's praises. "If I ever found myself in trouble with the law, Rose Markowitz is the one attorney I'd ever call." With complete trust in my uncle, I put Sonia Wilson's life in Ms. Markowitz's hands. The diminutive octogenarian criminal defense attorney extraordinaire turned out to be a superstar and saved Sonia Wilson's tush. She kicked the homicide detective's ass, and Sonia was out of jail before the fingerprint ink dried. Hopefully, she would do the same for Mo Mac. So far, Ms. Markowitz was still batting a thousand. Mo Mac should be so lucky. I crossed my fingers that Maureen Tyne wouldn't end Ms. Markowitz's winning streak.

Hope studied the Yenta's faces. "If it's not Mo Mac, then who?"

Queenie tapped her index finger on the tip of her nose. "Who had the most to lose?"

I spoke right up. "My vote goes to Carrie Le Beau. She forfeited a bright future at Clothing Concepts to follow Jack to Mermaid. She blames him for getting her fired." I glanced at the *West Coast Apparel News* headline. "Or, she wanted Jack to leave Mo Mac and he refused?"

Queenie shook her head. "Nah. If that's what she wanted, Carrie got her wish. Mo Mac threw Jack out of the house the night at Coast Pizza Parlor. He moved into Carrie's cottage the next day."

I said, "Lynnie said Carrie blamed Jack for her troubles. The spouse is always the first one the cops suspect, but AJ ought to take a closer look at Carrie before she throws the book at Maureen Tyne."

Sonia said, "What about your designer? Wasn't she furious at Jack for firing her?"

A suggestion so preposterous, it made me laugh. "Lynnie?" I tapped my cheek. "Nah. She's a gentle soul. She feeds the homeless and rescues shelter dogs. Besides, I convinced David to let me keep her with a glorified clerical job. She's a talented designer. Eventually, a competitor would have snatched her up. As it turned out, she was reinstated as our juniors division designer, so Lynnie is good. It's Carrie who hates Jack for ruining her life."

Joan wrinkled her forehead. "I hate to say it, but let's not leave out your vaunted leader. David is two steps from the board kicking him to the curb, and Jack's to blame."

I flexed my steepled fingers. "Better add Harvey Mazer, our chief financial officer, to the suspect list. The board is just as pissed at him because of Jack as they are at David."

Queenie burst out laughing. "Come on. Do you see either of those prima donnas getting their hands dirty *murdering someone*? Get real."

Right. At the same time, I get drafted by the NBA.

Sonia said matter-of-factly, "How about they hired a hitman?"

I puckered my lips. "Anything is possible, but I can't see it."

Hope shivered. "You guys went to Maureen's?"

Queenie's sigh broke my heart. "Afraid so."

The memory made me shudder. "A horrible situation. Maureen got arrested while still in her bathrobe. She had to beg AJ to let her get dressed before they took her into custody."

Sonia puckered her lips. "Was she handcuffed?"

Queenie's eyes went dark as a cavern. "Yeah." She spat. "Her arms behind her back, no less. At least her kids didn't witness their mother being led away in handcuffs."

Joan asked, "Any idea why they arrested Mo Mac?"

I scoffed. "Not a chance. AJ and the uniforms kept their mouths zipped tight. Several evidence bags left the house. No guess as to the contents."

Joan narrowed her eyes. "They must have given her an inventory."

Queenie's voice caught. "No. Detective Yakamura arrested her, and one of the uniforms read Mo Mac her rights."

Sonia asked, "So, is it bad?"

I bunched my shoulders. "Not great. Ms. Markowitz gave us the highlights. They confiscated a prescription of Jack's for acetaminophen COD 3. But the cops found blood-thinner pills for people who had AFIB inside the vial."

Hope asked, "Jack had a heart condition?"

I shook my head no. "No. And the problem is, no one in his family does either. Mo Mac said she had no idea know how those pills got into the vial. Ms. Markowitz said the police found an empty thermos Jack took to the beach with drops of juice and thallium poison coating the bottom. Jack left his stuff on the same spot at the beach every day. The police theorize Mo Mac followed Jack to the beach and put the poison in his thermos while he surfed every morning."

Sonia scrunched her face. "Makes no sense. If she wanted to poison him, why not put it into the thermos before he left home?"

Hope fanned her hands. "You're right. Why do it at the beach and risk being seen?"

I said, "There's a refrigerator in their garage with two containers of fruit juice laced with thallium poison inside. Mo Mac said the garage frig is strictly Jack's domain. He kept his energy drinks, beer, and his secret barbecue sauce in it. Neither the kids nor Mo Mac ever went into the refrigerator. Mo Mac told Ms. Markowitz she doesn't give her kids juice. It has too much sugar, and the kids bounce off the walls. She serves only fresh fruit. She swore she kept no juices inside the house, and she never put any of the juice the police found in the garage frig."

Queenie said, "The police also discovered a container of rat poison on a shelf in the garage."

Joan deadpanned. "Anything else?"

Queenie laughed a gallows laugh. "Oh, yeah. Let's not leave off the cherry from the sundae. The Tynes took out a million-dollar life insurance policy with a double indemnity clause if Jack died accidentally. Naturally, Mo Mac is the sole beneficiary."

Joan surveyed the table. "So, a few minor details. No worries. Piece of cake for a pro like Ms. M."

Yikes.

Chapter Fourteen

Queenie chugged the last of her scotch and waved her empty glass at the Bay Burger server. I took a fry out of the basket and used it as a pointer, but Queenie beat me to the punch, making my point. "Go ahead and say it. Ms. Markowitz says once the fingerprint and DNA tests come back, she's confident Mo Mac will be exonerated. But it better not take too much longer. Ms. M. visited Mo Mac today, and our girl isn't doing so hot."

I said, "Must be scary for her to sit in jail, especially for something she didn't do. But if anyone can get Mo Mac exonerated, my money is on Ms. M."

Queenie's eyes lit. "I shopped stores last night to get my mind off of this awful Mo Mac situation. Mira Kumar's line has an impressive four-way rack display right on the front aisle of the Bainbridge swim department. Boy, Mira's styling is spot on. She's taken sportswear bodies and put them into beachwear fabrics. And she's added matching swimsuits to the collection. Smart merchandising. Mira's updated styles go from the swimming pool to the carpool." Queenie clucked her tongue. "Our Sand & Sea cover-up styles are so dowdy compared to Mira's. Our styles are too basic and boring. And let's be honest, our designs haven't changed much in several seasons. Someone fashion-forward and innovative like Mira is exactly who we need."

I said, "It would be a ginormous change to make

from being her own boss to working for somebody else, but it doesn't hurt to test the waters and find out. If she keeps the styling different, maybe she could design for us and still keep her own line. It's kinda funny. A week ago, we didn't know her, and now she shows up everywhere we turn."

Queenie asked, "What do you mean?"

I said, "You looked at her line last night, and I ran into Mira today at a trim supplier. I arrived as Mira finished her appointment. Since they only needed my approvals for a few color tabs, my meeting took less than ten minutes. Mira waited for me, and we went for coffee afterward. She is as worried as we are for Mo Mac. She had an idea that might help. We told Ms. Markowitz to ask Mo Mac if the laundry was clean or dirty the days before Jack's death? And if not, was the laundry confiscated by the police? We found out the laundry was dirty, and Ms. M said it isn't on the list of confiscated items. Ms. M is going to ask AJ to test the laundry for traces of rat poison. It's risky. If rat poison is in the laundry, Mo Mac is toast. But if not, it helps knock a hole in AJ's theory."

Queenie drummed her fingers on the table. "Sitting around and waiting to see if it will happen doesn't work for me."

"Of course not." I grinned. "Fortunately, I've got an idea. AJ's needle is stuck on the theory Mo Mac poisoned the juice in Jack's thermos at the beach and not at home."

Queenie wrinkled her nose. "Sonia's comment was spot on. Why risk discovery? It doesn't make any sense. It's a lot smarter to add the poison to the juice before Jack filled the thermos."

I laughed. "Are you trying to help Mo Mac get outta jail or making it easier for AJ to keep her locked up forever? Lemme tell you my idea."

The Queenster narrowed her eyes. "If it involves any burgling, count me out. I've experienced enough near-death adventures to last me a lifetime."

To find evidence clearing Sonia Wilson of Bunny Frank's murder, Queenie and I had burgled the Clothing Concepts showroom a couple of times as well as CC sales executive Ronnie Schwartzman's yacht. So, ok, some parts of the capers weren't executed as smoothly as planned. But it's a mystery why Queenie's nose got so far out of joint. No bloodshed or handcuffs were involved. One or two minor hitches in the giddyap, max. No big freaking deal. Geesh.

I snickered. "Technically, it wasn't a burglary. We used a key." She opened her mouth to protest, but I waved her fears off by flicking a wrist. "Relax. No burgling. At least not yet. You're right, though, it doesn't make any sense. So, I've been thinking…"

Queenie crossed her index fingers into an X and groaned. "Uh-oh. Those are the most terrifying words in the English language."

I gave her the middle finger salute. "Pop and Andy, the other guy I see at the pier each morning, both remembered a couple who reminded them of Jack and Carrie at the beach every day. They said the couple took photos of one another on their phones. I printed photos of Jack, Carrie, Mo Mac, and Lynnie to run past Pop and Andy. If they identify Jack and Carrie, I'll tell AJ to see the photos on Jack and Carrie's phones. They will be date stamped and help prove Mo Mac didn't poison Jack at the beach."

Queenie made a sour face but grudgingly approved. "It's a start. It doesn't help the issue of the refrigerator in the garage, but at least it casts some doubt. Are you gonna do it soon?"

"Tomorrow morning." I wiggled my brows. "Wanna go? I'll even spring for coffee." I grinned evilly. "I'd pay a king's ransom to see you vertical before dawn. You can experience something new. See the sunrise. You may surprise yourself, and find it so enjoyable, you'll start walking every morning with Siggie and me."

Queenie waved me off and laughed. "Not a chance. God isn't out of bed that early, so neither am I."

****

I grabbed a couple of spoons and played a drumroll on the table. "The good news is Pop and Andy didn't recognize Lynnie and Mo Mac, but they picked out Jack and Carrie immediately."

Joan looked over the rim of her eyeglasses. "And the bad news?"

I giggled. "Pop hugged Mo Mac's picture to his chest and asked if I knew Carrie's *mother's* phone number."

Sonia scratched her head. "So, does this help Mo Mac?"

I smiled. "Yep. We've got two witnesses who are at the pier every day at the same time as Jack, who identified him and Carrie as being on the beach together. They confirm never seeing Mo Mac at the beach or on the pier at any time when Jack surfed. AJ might say Mo Mac went to the beach, found Jack's things, and put poison in his thermos while he surfed. But doing it out in the open is risky. And now, we have two witnesses who confirmed Mo Mac wasn't on the pier or the sand while

Jack surfed. At least, this punches a hole in AJ's theory."

Joan pinched her lips. "Ok, great, but she's not out of the woods yet. It still doesn't solve the problem of she didn't need to go to the beach to do it."

Queenie nodded. "True. Ms. Markowitz says it will all come down to comparing Mo Mac's fingerprints to the ones on the thermos, the refrigerator, the containers in the frig, the medication vial, and of course, the laundry rat-poison free."

Joan wiggled her digits in the air. "So, say she wore gloves."

I waggled my index finger. "Nope. If she wore gloves, the fingerprints already on the surfaces get smudged or wiped off altogether. According to Ms. Markowitz, the fingerprints on everything are clear, but no identity as to who they belong to yet."

Sonia said, "Mo Mac lives in the house. Her fingerprints will be on those things."

I nodded. "Logic says you're right, but Mo Mac said she never touched them."

Hope grimaced. "And the rat poison in the garage?"

A headshake discounted the question. "*Everyone* at the beach has a rat problem, so keeping rat poison is not unusual. The police are testing the poison in the garage. If there's no thallium in it, it's not the rat poison in Jack's system."

Hope said, "Suppose AJ says Mo Mac poisoned Jack with a rat poison containing thallium and ditched the container?"

I scoffed. "Let her suppose until the cows come home, but the evidence knife cuts both ways. Without any proof, her theory is a big nothing burger. She'd need to produce the rat poison containing thallium in Mo

Mac's possession. At the minimum, AJ needs receipts proving Mo Mac bought thallium. Snip says it is banned in this country and is virtually impossible to buy. Unless Mo Mac already had it, she'd have a heck of a time getting her hands on it."

Sonia said, "A life insurance policy on Jack naming Mo Mac as the sole beneficiary is extremely suspicious."

I gave Sonia the stink eye. "You've got two kids. Surely you have life insurance."

Sonia steepled her fingers. "Of course, I do, but my ex isn't the beneficiary. If I die and my kids are under eighteen, my oldest brother is the executor of my estate and distributes the insurance money."

Queenie wagged her index finger. "It's not like Mo Mac took out a huge life insurance policy on Jack with her as the sole beneficiary two days before Jack is murdered. It's not a new policy. It's seventeen years old. Jack and Mo Mac took the original policy out at the birth of their son and revised it with the birth of their daughter."

Joan bit her lip. "And all this goes...?"

I held up a napkin and wiped my fingers on it. "If the fingerprints don't match Mo Mac's, AJ will re-interview Pop and Andy and use the photos on Jack's phone to confirm Jack and Carrie as the couple they recognized at the beach. She is going to interview Carrie and examine the photos on her phone too."

Hope said, "Why the wait? Why isn't she doing everything now?"

I turned to Sonia. You want to take this one?"

Sonia took a deep bow. "AJ says the right suspect is already in custody."

Chapter Fifteen

The flush of embarrassment crept from the front of my neck to my scalp as the Yentas stood and gave me a coffee-mug salute.

Sonia's eyes shone. "You solved another one, Nancy Drew. Congratulations. You made Miss Marple proud."

Hope said, "I bet your picture hangs in the police station."

Sonia snorted. "On America's most wanted list."

Joan fondly cuffed my chin. "Yeah, America's most wanted pain in the tush."

I dipped my head. "I provided a few pictures to a couple of witnesses. It's Ms. Markowitz who deserves the kudos."

Queenie pointed her coffee cup at me. "Don't sell yourself short. Those eyewitnesses proved crucial. They blew a big hole in the detective's case."

I flashed my best aw-shucks smile. "I appreciate it, but science is how Mo Mac got off. The lab found no traces of rat poison in Mo Mac's laundry. And the rat poison in her garage had no thallium in it. The DNA swab Mo Mac volunteered sealed the deal. And as she predicted, her fingerprints weren't on any of the evidence. They ran the fingerprints through the system, but so far, they haven't had a single hit. AJ is back to square one."

Joan tapped my coffee cup with her spoon. "So, Nancy Drew, who's the culprit?"

I said, "My money is still on Carrie Le Beau, but I bet AJ will be at Mermaid any day now."

Queenie grimaced. "This ought to be fun."

Yeah. If you fancy a colonoscopy.

****

I stopped off at Lynnie's on the way back from David's to my office. "Hey, David gave me a heads-up on Detective Yakamura. She's coming to the factory later to question us." I joked, "If you've got anything incriminating, now's a good time to hide it."

****

Telephone, telegraph, tell Queenie. She came into my office with one of those expressions plastered across her kisser. No doubt she had a story to tell. Not a big surprise. Hardly a day goes by without a Queenie story.

The perennial question at Mermaid is which one of them—David's secretary Harriet, the mouth of Mermaid, or Queenie, the megaphone of the mart—is the bigger gossip?

Harriet Cowan sported bleach-blonde, big hair and had a sexy Mae West-hourglass figure that had started going to middle-aged plump. Fiftyish Harriet had been David's secretary for ten years. She bossed David around, not the reverse. But he never figured it out. Harriet ran the executive suite with the precision of a Marine drill sergeant. If you wanted to get *anything* done at Mermaid, Harriet is the go-to girl.

Queenie said, "I'm in Harriet's office confirming some figures before I turned in a sales report when the receptionist called to announce Detective Yakamura. Harriet excused herself, goes to reception, and brings AJ into David's office. You've been in Harriet's office. It's connected to David's via a pass-through door. It's not visible if you're sitting at the conference table. Detective Yakamura sat at the conference table across from David with her back to the pass-through. Harriet cracked the door open, and we overheard the entire interview. The interview started friendly enough. Detective Yakamura thanked David for meeting with her and vowed to keep the interview as brief as possible. The detective asked David if he and Jack worked together someplace else before here. And if not, how did Jack Tyne end up at Mermaid?"

An excellent question, since Jack appeared one day seemingly out of thin air.

Queenie said, "David explained, 'No, we never worked together anywhere else. Jack and I sat next to one another at a fashion show at the Miami swimwear market a few seasons ago. We shared some laughs and exchanged business cards, but we never spoke to one another again. Out of the clear blue, Jack called to say our juniors and kids products looked great in the stores, but we missed an important segment of the business by not having a surf line in our product mix. He said he had access to an iconic surf line and asked if we'd be interested in a licensing opportunity. We were already considering adding the category, so we asked him to make a presentation. The product impressed us and filled a hole in our product line. We met the GOOFYFOOT people, negotiated terms, and signed a licensing deal brokered by Jack.' AJ said, 'So, Mr. Tyne served as some sort of agent between the licensor and Mermaid. Once you signed the deal, did Mr. Tyne play any role going forward?' David told her our background is in a fashion product, not surf wear. Since Jack had experience in both categories, he hired Jack to run all our juniors and kids divisions. AJ asked for a list of Jack's responsibilities."

I laughed out loud. "Only one. Creating chaos."

Queenie crossed her eyes. "David gave her a list. Next, the detective asked David to characterize his relationship with Jack. She said, 'You and the victim were close, right, Mr. Workman? You and Mr. Tyne met for coffee every day.' "

AJ and I never discussed their morning coffee klatch. Those investigative skills are why they call her a detective.

Queenie said, "David tried to put a positive spin on it and still be as honest as he is capable of being." I gave her the big eyes, and Queenie laughed. "Yeah, I realize this lowers the bar quite a bit. David said they had coffee together every morning. David said he used the coffee time to get Jack in line. Jack marched to the beat of his own drum and often out of sync with the rest of our corporate band."

I smirked. "A big load of crap. Out of sync with the rest of us? He wished. Closer to not on the same level as us. A blowhard impressed with himself. When the rubber met the road, he turned out to be an incompetent who fast-talked himself into a job well beyond his capabilities."

Queenie nodded her agreement. "All true. AJ asked him to explain. David said there were a couple of challenges meshing Jack's ways and ours."

I scoffed. "Is he kidding? A *couple* of challenges?"

Queenie said, "AJ agreed. How'd she put it?" Queenie closed her eyes in concentration. "Oh yeah. The detective said, 'The level of job competence in every aspect of the work Mr. Tyne performed under your employ turned out to be nothing short of disastrous, right? Almost as though he deliberately set out to destroy your business. Mr. Tyne's incompetence cost your company a fortune. Weren't you furious at him?' "

I stroked my chin. "You'd think David would find it curious how she knew all the dirt. I would be."

Queenie tsked. "He didn't ask." Queenie clucked her tongue. "My guess? Mr. Big Shot Tough Guy wasn't prepared for the answer. He said he wasn't furious at Jack, just at himself for allowing it all to happen in the first place."

I rolled my eyes. "Such a crock. David went bonkers for the guy until Jack made him look bad."

Queenie said, "David said he should have put the brakes on Jack. AJ asked, 'So why didn't you?' "

I snarked. "Do I get the shovel out now?"

Queenie laughed. "Oh yeah. Better get the industrial-sized one. You're gonna need it. David called Jack Tyne the greatest talker he ever met. Every time David challenged Jack, his explanations sounded reasonable, and David bought them hook, line, and sinker. David said Jack Tyne told him one helluva great story, and now he'd been fooled by the best."

I made the international gag sign. "Hold on. You're right. I need a much bigger shovel. Better yet, a front loader. AJ buy any of David's huge wad of crap?"

Queenie laughed. "Not much. AJ told David before she even called to schedule their interview, she spoke to the board members." Queenie shuddered. "She got quite an earful from Earl Bernard."

I mused out loud. "Are the board members suspects?"

Queenie's bugged eyes said I'd grown a set of horns.

I jutted my jaw. "Don't turn your nose up at the suggestion. Earl and the board are furious at Jack. Earl owns an exterminating company. Maybe he exterminated Jack along with the rats."

Queenie gave me the stink eye. "Hardly. The board made it crystal clear they are super pissed at David and Harvey. AJ discussed their probation, their salary cuts, and their termination if they don't get the company profits back, and the clock is ticking."

I patted my cheeks. "Good grief! How'd David react to being called out and his nose rubbed in it to boot by the police?"

Queenie pursed her lips. "Like you'd expect. Fit to be tied."

I said, "David and Harvey are no angels, but for the sake of argument, murdering Jack helps them how? Firing Jack made a lot more sense than killing him."

Queenie bunched her shoulders. "Dunno. The detective asked David if he suffered from a heart condition and brought up the rat problems. Some of the questions came from out of the left field. I guess she was poking around for a reaction?"

I grinned. "I bet she got one."

Queenie traced a finger across her forehead. "Oh yeah. Major league big time. The vein in the middle of his forehead danced an Irish jig." Queenie gave me the big eyes. "David says to her, 'Your stupid questions are nothing but poppycock. First, you're concerned if I've got a bad ticker. Now you ask if my building is infested with rats.' He says he didn't have the patience or interest in idiotic questions. He stood and said, 'If you've got nothing germane to ask, I'm due at a meeting in five minutes. My assistant will see you out." Queenie widened her eyes. "The detective told him to sit down and *shut up*. She said she didn't care one hoot for his opinion of her questions, but he better answer them, and he better plan on being late for the next meeting. And for the record, she decides if and when their meeting is finished, not him."

AJ is not easily intimidated, but David isn't one easily pushed around. I leaned forward in my seat. "And she wasn't shown the door?"

Queenie's husky voice rose twenty octaves. "Amazingly, no. Either he didn't realize he could tell her to get lost, or he was too scared to throw her out. He tells her his heart is fine and the rat problem is resolved. She asks Mr. Workman, 'Can you account for your whereabouts the day Mr. Tyne died?' David waved around his office. So, AJ asks David to prove it. David said, 'Let's see you prove I can't.' "

Good grief. Was the guy plumb dumb or just arrogant? Toss a coin. "Was he arrested?"

Queenie sighed. "No, but the detective wasn't too kicked in the ass with David's attitude or his BS answers one bit."

I smiled grimly. "I guarantee Detective Yakamura is far from done with David Workman."

Chapter Sixteen

Two days later, Queenie and I pulled into our factory's double driveway and barely missed hitting a lamppost. I stared gape-mouthed at the dozen LAPD squad cars blocking the entrance to the building.

Queenie screeched loud enough to raise the dead. "OMG! It happened to us now. We've been robbed. A string of daytime robberies of garment factories has plagued the area recently." Queenie slapped her cheeks. "My friend Ann at Fortune Cookies said their place got hit last month. Five heavily armed guys wearing Halloween masks backed a step van into the Fortune Cookies loading dock and cleaned the warehouse out in ten minutes. They lost at least a quarter of a million dollars' worth of inventory."

I pointed to the faded red sedan. "Forget being robbed. We should be so lucky. AJ's car is parked next to David's. She's not investigating a robbery. We've got much bigger problems. She's investigating Jack's murder."

We found Harriet Cowan in the lobby muttering to herself and walking in a continuous figure-eight. I caught David's secretary as she made the turn and blocked her path. "Harriet, what's going on?"

Harriet wrung her hands and gulped. "Your friend the detective and an army of uniforms marched in at seven forty-five. The detective waved a search warrant,

91

itching to serve it." A nervous giggle escaped from Harriet's lips. "The new receptionist started today. Monica got a gander at the cop's guns, and I bet she wet her pants."

I glanced at the reception desk. No kidding. The mousy-looking puddle of nerves twitched every time the phone lines rang. I angled my head at Monica and smirked. "Let's see if she comes to work tomorrow."

Queenie cocked a brow. "I wouldn't make book on it."

I turned to Harriet. "Who was the warrant served to?"

Harriet took a deep breath. "The detective wanted to serve the warrant to either David or Harvey, but neither of them had come in yet. The only employees in the building were Monica, Lynnie Stubbs, the sample sewers, the warehouse crew, and me. As the most senior one available, I got the honors."

Queenie wrinkled her nose. "What are they searching for?"

Harriet shook her head, and the platinum hair teased into a poufy bouffant shifted from side to side. "I dunno. The warrant said nothing specific. A blanket court order giving them the authority to search the entire facility and confiscate anything they deemed questionable."

I said, "David's car is in his parking space. Is he in his office?"

Harriet wrung her hands. "No. The detective wouldn't let David stay in his office while the police searched it."

Queenie's eyes widened as big as two saucers. "They're searching in *David's* office?"

Harriet said, "The detective made it clear the search

encompassed the entire building. David's office is no exception."

I gave her the big eyes. "Bet he made one heck of a fuss. It's a wonder he wasn't arrested."

Harriet shuddered. "It came perilously close to happening. I pushed David kicking and yelling into Harvey's office. I told Harvey to bar the door, if necessary, but not to let David out, or the detective might cuff him to a chair."

I glanced at my watch. Ten thirty. At this rate, the search could last all day. Unbelievable. "Will they let us go into our offices, or are they searching them too?"

Harriet shook her head. "Nope. The detective made me announce on the PA for everyone to go into the lunchroom until the police completed their search. She made David and Harvey go to the lunchroom too. They searched my office first and even made Monica move. They cleared the two of us, and we're the only ones exempt from waiting in the lunchroom."

I asked, "Including the production and shipping staff?"

Harriet nodded. "No one is exempt."

I frowned. "The lunchroom is huge, but it's not big enough to hold all those people at the same time."

Harriet nodded. "You're right. I pointed that out to the detective. All the production and distribution staff are waiting outside the warehouse next to the loading dock."

Queenie asked, "How much longer?"

Harriet made a sour face. "Dunno. The detective said she'd let me know when they completed the search."

I pointed to the hall leading to the lunchroom. "Should we go to the lunchroom?"

Before Harriet replied, AJ and six uniforms carrying

evidence bags walked into the lobby. The uniforms took the evidence bags out of the building, and AJ turned to Harriet. "We've completed our search. Please ask Mr. Workman to meet me in his office." AJ cocked a brow. "Tell him to behave himself. I'm in no mood for any more of his shenanigans."

****

Queenie, Harriet, and I crammed ourselves into Harriet's tiny office. Harriet cracked the pass-way door open. A grim-faced uniformed policeman stood at attention inside the office across from the conference table, blocking David's closed door. Did the cop think David planned to escape? David Workman, a fugitive from the law? A laughable concept, but LAPD was taking no chances.

AJ sat across from David at his conference table. She wore thin surgical gloves, and a blazing expression burned deep in her dark eyes. A container labeled Superb Shine Car Soap and a small prescription-sized vial sat on the conference table.

David pointed to the car soap container. "Where was this? I've been hunting high and low for it."

AJ pointed diagonally across the room and pursed her lips. "Exactly in the place you hid it. Wrapped in a terrycloth towel under a dozen swimsuits in the bottom of a carton in the back of your closet."

David's voice rose to a soprano on crack. "Are you insane? I didn't hide it! I've gone crazy trying to *find* it. I get my car washed and detailed every Friday, but I hate the cheap soap Diego uses." David pointed to the container. "This stuff prevents surface scratches and leaves no spots or stains." David laughed. "Diego will be thrilled. He won't hear me crabbing about the streaks his lousy soap leaves this week."

AJ asked. "You said this building had a rat infestation, right?"

David nodded. "Yes, we did. But an exterminator came out, and the rats are gone now. Why?'

AJ put the container in front of David. "If the rat problem is no longer an issue, why keep rat poison in your closet? Why hide it wrapped in a swimsuit hidden in a carton? Please help me understand, Mr. Workman. I'm at a loss, so enlighten me."

David jerked back as though AJ pushed a live grenade in his face. David screeched loudly enough to raise the dead. "*Rat poison*? Are you deaf, or are you dumb? This is a container of car soap. *Car soap*, not rat poison!"

AJ scoffed. "The *label says* car soap. The *contents inside* the container remain to be determined." AJ put the container back on the table and grabbed the vial. "We found this in your bottom drawer. Care to explain them?"

David thinned his lips. "I keep some Tylenol and my vitamins in the vial."

AJ dipped her head. "Why keep them in an unmarked vial? Why not in the jars the pills came in?"

David rolled his eyes. "We buy them at PRICECO. The economy-size jars the pills came in are huge. They won't fit in my desk drawer. When I run out, I refill the vial. Why all the pill questions?"

AJ stared coldly at David's perspiring face. "Let me explain the way police interviews are conducted, Mr. Workman. *I* ask the questions, and *you* answer them."

AJ fingered the vial. "You said you don't have a heart condition."

David nodded. "Right."

AJ made a note. "Anyone in your family?"

David shook his head. "Nope."

AJ scowled. "Mr. Workman, you do realize that's easy to check?"

David snapped, "Check all you want. I am telling you. No one in my family has a bad ticker."

AJ put a tissue on the table and spilled the pills onto it. "Do you see any Tylenol? Do you see any vitamins? These are prescription pills."

David said, "I take no prescription medications."

AJ's smile was colder than a Chicago January blizzard. "So, I'm quite curious why a vial of prescription medication is in your desk drawer."

David shrugged. "Your guess is as good as mine."

AJ pointed to the vial. "And you take your pills every day?"

David took a few moments. "I take Tylenol for a headache, but the vitamins?" David laughed. "If I remember to take them. Yeah. Every day."

AJ's voice dripped sarcasm. "And *miraculously*, you never noticed your pills not being in the vial? Not worried you'd taken some unidentified medication with who knows what kind of side effect? I find it hard to believe. Mr. Workman."

David shrugged. "It's been crazy here. I can't remember if I ate lunch yesterday, let alone the last time I took a vitamin."

AJ snarked. "If things were so crazy, you probably needed extra-strength aspirin."

David massaged his temples. "Not the type of headaches aspirin fixes."

AJ pointed to the vial. "No idea at all how these got in the vial?" AJ scoffed. "The medicine fairy dropped it into your desk drawer in case you need it for some unidentified malady someday?"

David shrugged. "I can't tell you."

AJ sneered, "BS. Since *you* put them in the vial, why not?"

David spat each word rat-a-tat-tat like bullets shot from a machine gun. "I. Have. No. Idea."

AJ glared. "Can't or won't say?"

David held out his hands. "I told you. I've never seen them before. What's in them?"

AJ sneered. "We found them in your drawer. You tell me."

David banged his fist so hard, the vial tipped over, and the pills spilled onto the table. "Are you deaf or dumb, or can't you understand English? How many times must I say it?"

AJ put a palm out to stop the uniform who approached the table with his fingers wrapped around the grip of his service revolver. "You're not helping yourself, Mr. Workman."

David raked his hair until it stood up on end at the angle of a rooster's comb. "Obviously, someone removed my pills, substituted those, and put the vial back in my desk drawer."

AJ pursed her lips. "And who does such a thing?"

David raised his arms to the ceiling. "Obviously, someone who wants to frame me."

AJ asked, "Frame you for what?"

David snapped. "For whatever it is you think I did."

AJ sneered. "Why pick you to frame?"

David held open his palms. "I pissed somebody off? I dunno. Your guess is as good as mine."

AJ said, "You don't seem to know much, Mr.

Workman, so let me help you out. You poisoned Jack Tyne. Mr. Tyne's business proved such a disaster, the board threatened to fire you if you didn't clean up his mess." AJ leaned across the table and invaded David's space. "If you didn't get rid of him, Jack Tyne destroys your career, so you killed him. You and the victim met in your office for coffee together every morning. Before he came in, you spiked a cocktail of rat poison and blood thinner in his coffee. And it worked. Mr. Tyne's gums started bleeding, and his hair began falling out in tufts. Those are classic signs of thallium-laced rat poisoning."

David scoffed. "Why kill him? We planned to fire him. He put fake orders in the system, and we are stuck with a warehouse full of his unsold goods." David laughed. "He did us a favor and died before we fired him. Saved us a bundle in severance and unemployment."

AJ said, "His screw-ups cost your company a fortune in lost profits and brought your career to the brink of destruction. You stood to lose everything you worked so hard for, and you blamed Jack Tyne for it all. No, Mr. Workman, firing Jack Tyne wasn't enough for you. You wanted to punish him. You wanted him dead. But you wanted him to suffer. So, you poisoned him. Slowly, daily, in his morning coffee. So, the poison you fed him destroyed him by eating at his insides, day by day."

David's jaw dropped. "You're outta your mind, lady."

AJ shook her head no. "No, I'm not. We're gonna test the pills and the contents of the container. We're gonna find blood thinner pills in a vial and a container of rat poison with your fingerprints on them."

David turned white as a ghost. "Do I need a

lawyer?"

AJ smiled like a shark. "You tell me, Mr. Workman. Do you?"

****

"Lynnie," I asked as she paced back and forth. "Calmly, tell me again."

Lynnie nervously shredded her tissue and shook her head. "I came in extra early to finish the Maxmart presentation. I'm under the gun. I'm rushing to put the samples and swatches together to make the morning pickup. All of a sudden, this lady cop marches in, waving a badge and shoves a piece of paper under my nose. She orders me out of my office while two uniforms search it."

Lynnie balled a fist to swipe at the tears leaking out of the corners of her eyes. "I wait in the lunchroom with everyone else for an hour. She finally lets me back into my office and asks if I have AFIB and do I take some X-named medication or something. I've no idea what AFIB is, and I am certainly not familiar with the medication."

Lynnie stopped pacing long enough to take a new tissue out of the box on her desk. She wiped her red nose on the tissue and honked into it, making the sound of a tinny car horn.

Like a two-legged metronome, she resumed her pacing. She shuddered. "She asked the same questions again and again in a bunch of different ways, trying to trip me. And such crazy questions. Isn't it a fact I wanted to get back at David for letting Jack fire me? Didn't I hate Jack for firing me before giving me a chance to prove myself? Didn't I want to get even? Didn't I blame him for tanking my career? Didn't I blame him for my menial job? Didn't I blame him for my money troubles?

Didn't I try to sabotage his lines? Didn't I want his division to fail? Didn't I want to make him pay for firing me for no reason?"

I dipped my head. "Lynnie, Detective Yakamura is a friend of mine. She's a good cop. She's fair. All she's trying to do is her job. To find the truth and get justice for Jack."

Lynnie wrung her hands. "Out of the blue, she asked if I lived at the beach. I told her no. I live in a canyon in the Santa Monica mountains. Then she asked if rats are a problem?" Lynnie gurgled a strangled laugh. "I said we have no rats, but the raccoons raiding the garbage bins are a real pain in the patootie." Lynnie raked her dark curly hair. "She said if Jack did to her what he did to me, she'd want him dead and didn't I too?" Lynnie's voice cracked. "The cop thinks I killed Jack! She said I had the big three: means, motive, and opportunity." Lynnie's eyes filled, and the pleading in her voice broke my heart. "Boss, promise that you believe me. Nothing she accused me of is true."

I smiled. "Trust me, she wasn't specifically targeting you. She's being thorough. You weren't singled out. She interviewed all of us: David, Harvey, Ike, Queenie, Harriet, the new receptionist, every sample sewer, and all the shipping clerks. She questioned everyone, including me." I smiled. "She even asked Bernice some pretty crazy questions."

Lynnie sniffled. "Bernice? Our Bernice?" Lynnie burst out laughing. "How did she think our head patternmaker killed Jack? By measuring him to death?"

I said, "The police searched your office. They searched the design studio and the test lab too, right?"

Lynnie nodded yes. "From what I've heard, they

searched every inch of the building. Why?"

I asked, "Was any evidence found pointing to you? Anything on your desk? The storage rooms? The design studio? The lab?"

Lynnie shook her head no. "Of course not. I had nothing incriminating for them to find." She quirked a lopsided sweet smile. "Besides, don't you remember? You alerted me the last time. You told me to expect the detective and, if I had anything incriminating, to get rid of it."

Chapter Seventeen

Clammy fingers of fog wrapped themselves around the shoulders of the early morning beachcombers as though a damp shroud. The brisk offshore wind nudged the Washington Street pier awake. It was high tide. The battered wooden pilings groaned their objections as the white caps mercilessly lashed against them.

The briny air had a sharp tang to it as Siggie, Queenie, and I stepped onto the cold, hard-packed sand. Mo Mac scheduled Jack Tyne's memorial at morning's first light. I checked my watch. A few more minutes until the memorial began. I let Siggie run up and down the beach until the pale sun struggled to rise. Its rim barely visible on the eastern horizon, the celestial interloper pushed itself into the morning. The orb fought for its place in an overcast, foggy gray sky the color of a rusted battleship as the small group of mourners gathered to say farewell to Jack Tyne.

A dozen wetsuit-clad inner-city Urban Surfers arrived to pay last respects to their sponsor. At the crack of dawn, each surfer carried their board from the sandy dunes to the foggy shoreline. They performed a "paddle out" for the "senior citizen" surfer they fondly called geezer. They paddled five hundred yards out to Jack's favorite spot and formed their boards into a circle. The surfers took their leis off and tossed them into the center of the circle. The biggest, burliest surfer positioned at the apex of the circle took a conch shell out of the goody bag hanging on his nylon utility belt and blew it loudly twice. The terns and seagulls flying overhead joined in the noisy salute. All twelve surfers raised a right fist to the sky and yelled *Cowabunga, Dude*. Then they fell into line behind the conch blower and paddled back to shore.

A moving tribute for a man most considered undeserving of the honor. An unfaithful husband, an inadequate father, and an unscrupulous con man. Jack Tyne had few accomplishments in his life to be proud of. But his tireless work for the inner-city Urban Surfers charity helped change the course of many kids' lives from one destined to be on the road to a dead end to one with a chance for a future. If Jack Tyne begged forgiveness for his sins, his dedication to the Urban Surfers served as his redemption ticket.

A dozen lit tiki lamps were set in a large circle above the berm. The Beach Boys' "Surfin' USA" blared a fitting introduction on a boom box in the background as the Urban Surfers entered the tiki circle. They jammed the noses of their boards into the sand in a diagonal line across the circle, splitting it in half. Then the Urban Surfers positioned themselves around the outer rim of the circle, standing at attention between the tiki lamps.

Next, Jack Tyne's children entered the circle and set his surfboard in the center of the line, nose into the sand. Jack's kids came to the memorial dressed from head to toe in GOOFYFOOT regalia. Jack's son was a taller, younger version of his father. His daughter was a thinner, more athletic image of Mo Mac as a young girl.

AJ Yakamura and I mouthed good morning to one another as she stood respectfully off to the side, not far from Pop and Andy. David, Harriet, Harvey, Ike, and

Bernice huddled together next to Queenie and me. Queenie sipped her coffee and shivered. "I still can't believe you and Mo Mac talked me into this." She glanced at the fog-laden gunmetal-gray sky. "The sky is still dark. God is still asleep at this ungodly hour." Queenie's tone shrilled incredulously. "And you do this *every* day?"

I deadpanned. "I do a round trip from the houseboat to the pier and back every morning. Today's the first memorial."

Queenie narrowed her eyes. "I better get triple points for this." She pulled her nylon jacket tighter and wrapped her arms around Siggie's neck for warmth. "No one on two legs should be outdoors this early."

Siggie woofed and kicked up some sand. Atta boy. You tell her, Sig. Good grief. The woman turned out to be a blue-ribbon whiner. "Do you expect a medal for getting your ass out of bed early? For crying out loud, put a cork in it already. I bought you a ginormous cup of coffee. Take a few big slurps and join the rest of humanity." I dipped my head to Jack's family standing together in stoic silence. "Buck up and shut up. You're here to support Mo Mac and her family. And"—I grinned—"to check out all the suspects."

Queenie's sleep-deprived, droopy eyes snapped wide open to attention. "Suspects?" She surveyed our little gathering and laughed. "Who? Bernice and Ike? Oh, yeah. They're definitely on America's most wanted list. A regular Bonnie and Clyde."

I rolled my eyes. "Not them, you dolt." I elbowed her in the ribs. "See the others? To the left of Ike's head over on the beachside of the berm. Isn't Carrie standing next to Lynnie?"

Queenie followed my eyes. "It's hard to tell. It's so foggy, I can't see my hand in front of my nose."

I squinted into the fog, rolling in from the shoreline to the berm. "Yeah, it's her."

AJ's sharp eyes scoured the crowd, observing all the mourners, but her peepers returned to David several times. I dipped my head in the detective's direction. "I bet AJ is mentally measuring David for a prison uniform. If she is considering David, she ought to look at Harvey too. He had as much to lose as David."

Queenie pointed at my to-go cup. "You drinking something stronger than coffee?"

I made a sour face. "Funny. If you enjoy having an appendectomy. Carrie is still my first choice. She gets my vote in the whodunit contestant search. According to Lynnie, Carrie isn't exactly heartbroken Jack is dead. She blames Jack for all her problems. Carrie lives at the beach, so there must be rat poison at her house. Carrie and Jack were inseparable. She had plenty of opportunities to add a splash of rat poison to Jack's morning java. She's got some nerve coming here. Mo Mac made it crystal clear Carrie was unwanted at the memorial." I glanced at Jack's widow. "I wonder if Mo Mac sees Carrie?"

Queenie gulped. "Crap, I hope not. This shindig is already weird enough. The last thing it needs is a catfight."

I tipped my head to the detective shivering in the dark dampness. "If Mo Mac sees Carrie, it's a good thing AJ is around." I grabbed Queenie's arm. "Come on, let's mingle."

Queenie snorted. "Mingle? This is a memorial, not a cocktail party."

I crossed my eyes and pulled her along to the other end of the gathering. I sidled next to Carrie and gave her the big eyes. "Surprised to see you here."

Carrie raised her brows. "Why? I came to pay my respects along with everyone else."

I shook my head no. "No, Mrs. Tyne *invited* everyone else. Mrs. Tyne specifically told *you* not to come. If you had really wanted to pay your respects, you would have respected Mrs. Tyne's wishes." I gave her the once-over. "So, come to make sure Jack's really dead?"

Carrie recoiled as though she'd been struck. "That's a horrible thing to say."

I cocked a brow. "Is it? Word is you're not taking Jack's death too hard." Carrie gave Lynnie a dirty look. "You blame Jack for ruining your career."

Carrie stuck her lower lip out, pathetic as a pouting toddler. "He did."

I snarked. "So, you paid him back by sprinkling a few drops of arsenic in his old lace, so to speak?"

Carrie snapped. "Who the hell do you think you are, talking to me like that? I won't take this crap from you."

The curly fur on Siggie's back flattened. Carrie eyed my pooch warily when he growled at her from deep in the back of his throat. Carrie moved to Lynnie's other side after Carrie tried vainly to make nice to Siggie. My canine confidant made his opinion of Carrie clear when he set his ears down into a fighting position and bared his teeth.

A hush fell over the mourners as the music stopped. Jack's widow entered the center of the circle. Mo Mac's eyes appeared clear but red-rimmed as she wrapped her arms around her children and addressed the group of mourners. "My children and I appreciate all of you coming out so early to help us celebrate Jack's life and give him a proper sendoff to ride the big wave to the other side." Mo Mac glanced at the Urban Surfers and quirked a sad smile. "Let's face it, Jack Tyne had his good moments, but he was no angel. But Jack's constant? His love for the eternal ocean of life." Mo Mac's voice cracked as she pulled her children closer. "While we grieve Jack's passing, we take solace he died doing the thing he loved the most. Jack's children chose special ways to say goodbye to their father. Megan will recite a poem she wrote, and JJ will play his rendition of 'Surfin' Safari' on his guitar."

When the children finished, Maureen beamed a beatific smile to the mourners. "Thank you again for coming to honor Jack." Maureen turned a three-sixty and surveyed the mourners. "Does anyone else care to share something?"

Carrie's hand shot up half-cocked when she and Mo Mac locked eyes. I pressed my palm on Carrie's arm and hissed low as a snake ready to strike. "Don't even try it."

Carrie scoffed. "Why? Are you gonna call a cop?"

I pointed to AJ. "Nah, I'll wave, and she'll come over." Carrie turned on her heel and stomped past the berm as the Urban Surfers faced the ocean. They lifted their surfboards above their heads and saluted Jack Tyne a final time.

Cowabunga, Dude.

Chapter Eighteen

David had turned the management meeting over to Harvey a tortuously long hour ago. Harvey's jaws must ache from his nonstop yakking. In his efforts to save the company from financial ruin, Harvey risked boring it to death with his yammering about pie charts and the best ways to increase our return on investment.

Right in the middle of Harvey explaining the dire implications of the fiftieth pie chart, the door to David's office swung open. AJ Yakamura and two LAPD uniforms barged into the room. The normally unflappable Harriet Cowan paled white as a sheet as she stood between AJ and the boss. "D-David, I'm s-so sorry. I-I t-tried to s-stop her. I-I said you were in a meeting and told her to come back later. She said whatever you were doing wasn't important. She said whatever it was, you'd have to stop."

David glared at AJ. "How dare you interrupt us. Can't you see we're in the middle of a meeting?" David spat his disdain. "You're the police, not the Gestapo." David pointed to Harriet. "Make an appointment like everyone else. My secretary Harriet will give you my open time slots. Now, if you'll excuse us, we need to get back to our meeting."

AJ signaled the uniforms to get into position with a dip of her head. "Your meeting is over, Mr. Workman. Stand up." Along with the rest of us, David stared at AJ, slack-jawed. "David Workman, you are under arrest for the murder of Jack Tyne."

AJ motioned to the older one of the uniforms. "Mr. Workman, the officer will read you your rights. If you come quietly, I won't have the officer cuff you. Your choice: You can do this civilized or make a scene. But whichever way you choose, understand this. You're coming with us right now."

Cripes. I glanced at Harvey and shuddered. If dreaming of pie charts with our CFO leading the next management meeting was to be avoided, I better start poking around and find Jack's real killer pretty fast. Piece of cake. As if.

****

Word of David's arrest blazed through the California Apparel Mart at the speed of a wildfire. The shaken swimwear industry turned to those of us professionally closest to David for answers. We were inundated with so many calls that by mid-afternoon, I took the phone off the hook.

Morbidly curious as the rest of the industry, the Yentas battered us with questions the next morning.

Sonia's eyes bugged. "So, the police barged into the middle of a staff meeting to arrest *your boss*?"

I gave her the thumbs up. "Oh yeah, big time. AJ and two uniforms muscled into David's office despite his secretary's objections. It was pretty intense. Like a scene right out of *Law and Order*. If they'd drawn their guns, I'd probably peed myself."

Queenie laughed. "Or fainted."

Hope patted my wrist. "They arrested your boss *in front* of his employees? How mortifying for him."

Queenie smirked. "Nah. Normally, David's too

arrogant to get embarrassed so easily. This time? He was too busy wetting his pants."

Sonia shuddered. "Was he handcuffed the same as Martinez cuffed me?"

I waved the idea off with a flip of a wrist. "No. AJ said if he didn't want to be cuffed, he better behave. For once, David listened."

Sonia asked, "Ms. Markowitz able to meet him at the police station?"

I shook my head no. "Uh-uh. Ms. M. isn't who they hired."

Sonia's jaw dropped. "Why not? The woman makes Clarence Darrow seem like an amateur."

I shrugged. "Before AJ escorted David out, he told his secretary to call his wife and ask her brother to meet him at the precinct."

Sonia asked, "His brother-in-law is a criminal lawyer?"

I shook my head no. "Nope. He's a will and trusts attorney. His office is in the building next to my uncle Barry's in Beverly Hills."

Sonia dipped her head. "Wills and trusts? Your boss *does realize* the heap of trouble he's in, doesn't he?"

Hope lifted a shoulder. "If a criminal attorney wasn't necessary, maybe he's not in so much trouble."

I waved an index finger. "No, he's in a lot of trouble, and he is painfully aware of it. His brother-in-law went to protect him until a criminal attorney was hired. Our company's insurance policy for key executive employees like David and Harvey includes attorney fees. David's secretary said the firm hired a criminal attorney for him."

Sonia asked, "So, the container was filled with rat

poison, and the pills were blood thinners?"

I shrugged. "Since David got arrested, I'd say yes to both. David admitted the containers were his. They must be covered with his fingerprints."

Queenie clucked her tongue. "Detective Yakamura isn't playing around. Her case must be pretty solid."

Sonia pointed a teaspoon at me. "So, Nancy Drew, your take?"

I drummed my fingers on the edge of the table. "AJ's case against David is a bit too pat. Somebody went to a lot of trouble to frame him. Carrie Le Beau still gets my vote."

Hope asked, "And Siggie concurs?"

I grinned. "Siggie growled at Carrie when I questioned her at Jack's memorial, so, yep, he agrees."

Joan squirmed in her seat. "It's gonna sound awful coming from one of his own, but maybe he's guilty?" Joan turned to Queenie. "What is it you usually ask?"

Queenie replied, "Who has the most to lose?"

I ticked off a list of suspects. "Carrie Le Beau for sure. Harvey Mazer, our CFO, has as much to lose as David. Harvey is a CPA. He risks losing his license. His job, for sure. Maybe even his career. David is no choir boy, but he's not an idiot either. If he poisoned Jack's coffee, is he dumb enough to hide the evidence in his office?"

Joan's eyes glittered. "Dumb? Not a chance. Arrogant enough to think he could pull it off? Absolutely."

Chapter Nineteen

I studied Queenie from behind the rim of my wineglass. "Was your interpretation of Joan's response to my question the same as mine?"

Queenie drummed her fingertips on the table. "Remind me. Your nana always said…?"

I grinned. "Arrogance will kill you every time."

Queenie smiled sweetly. "Such a wise woman, your nana."

I agreed. "The wisest."

Queenie squared her shoulders. "My answer to your question? *No one* beats David Workman in the category of arrogance."

I smiled like a shark. "Oh, but you are wrong, my Queen. Indeed, someone else does."

Queenie's surprised eyes widened. "Who?"

I twirled a ta-da with my hands. "Ronnie Schwartzman."

Once one of the most powerful people in the swimwear industry, golden boy Ronnie Schwartzman did anything he wanted to and suffered no consequence. Ronnie's cushy world disintegrated when the brash Clothing Concepts sales executive murdered a prominent, powerful swimwear buyer. Now Ronnie is a long-term guest of the state at the Graybar hotel. It's a pay-me-now-or-pay-me-later world, but eventually, we all pay for our sins. Ronnie's sins cost him his freedom.

The buyer's sins cost the woman her life.

Queenie clucked her tongue. "No, smartass, name someone not in prison for life."

I said, "You're wrong. He's *exactly* the right person. Ronnie is the epitome of arrogance. And where did his get him? A permanent address at the state pen. So, tell me. Do you *honestly* think our boss poisoned Jack Tyne?"

Queenie tapped her index finger on the tip of her nose. "Honestly, no. I can't see him doing the deed."

I asked, "Why? Jack certainly gave him enough motivation."

Queenie tsked. "David doesn't have it in him. David's a big bully who yells at, embarrasses, and intimidates his underlings and leaves no doubt he's the boss. But David is a gutless wonder. He schemes and cheats and does underhanded things, but dirty his hands? Nah. Not a chance."

I laughed. "So, I guess David isn't one of your favorite people."

Queenie shrugged. "It's complicated. Ours is a love-hate relationship. He gave me my first big break in the industry, and I'll be forever grateful. But I've got no illusions. He only helped me to advance his own professional goals, not mine. As long as you understand David is first, foremost, and only for David, you'll be ok. If you're expecting him to be someone to depend on and trust to cover your back if the going gets tough, you're gonna be sorely disappointed."

I joked. "So, he's a first-class jerk, but not a killer."

Queenie cackled. "Exactly."

I dipped my head. "Then somebody worked awfully hard to frame him."

She narrowed her eyes. "Who?"

I said, "Using your theory of who has the most to lose, I vote for either Harvey or Carrie."

Queenie sputtered like a motor missing a cylinder. "H-Harvey M-Mazer? The n-nerdy n-numbers jockey whose pie charts put us to sleep?

I crossed my eyes. "Well, it's not Harvey, the six-foot-tall rabbit."

Queenie's hands flew to her heart as she gasped. "You're joking."

I shook my head no. "No, I'm not. Why are you so surprised? Harvey has as much to lose as David, maybe even more."

She eyed me as if measuring my torso for a straitjacket. "On which planet do you figure *more*?"

I held out my hands. "Bean counters are a dime a dozen and not difficult to replace. Whether you love him or hate him, the fact remains. David Workman is the face of the company. The board doesn't respect or trust David, but since he *is* the company in the eyes of the industry, the board is stuck with him. Harvey and the board are numbers people. They talk the same language. They understand one another. The board members are pissed at Harvey for allowing David to give Jack free rein, but Harvey still has the board's ear. They hear the things he wants them to hear. It's the figures *he* gives them they live or die on."

Queenie smirked. "Yeah, and it's his figures the board is furious about."

I held out my hands. "*Honest* figures, not manipulated ones, and ones the board blames David for."

Queenie bit her lip. "I still don't see how you get from pie charts and figures on a spreadsheet to Harvey framed David for murder."

Good grief! She must need a white-tipped cane to be this blind. "David allowed Jack to do stuff he'd fire anyone else for doing. David's a liability for Harvey as well as the board. But David is a necessary millstone around their necks. Can you think of a better means to get rid of David than framing him for murder? Harvey lives in a beachfront house in Playa del Rey, so he's got rat poison. David and Jack met in David's office for coffee every morning. Harvey gets to the office an hour before David. It's no secret David never locks his office. Say Harvey goes into David's office before anyone else is in and puts a few drops of rat poison into the GOOFYFOOT mug Jack kept in David's office."

Queenie laughed, "If Harvey wanted David gone, why poison Jack? Why not poison David?"

I needed her help, so I tamped back my impatience. "One stone kills two birds, and he gets rid of them both. Harvey's been in David's office often enough to see him take the car soap out of his closet to give to the guy who details his car. At some point, David took pills in front of Harvey, so the vial's location isn't a secret either. Not hard for Harvey to substitute the pills and the car soap and hide the containers for the cops to find."

Queenie wrinkled her brow. "I dunno. I suppose it's possible. But wrap my arms around it? Sorry, no can do."

I held out my hands. "Hey, I am not one hundred percent sold on Harvey either, but he's certainly worth a closer look, and so is Carrie. She also had the means, motive, and opportunity."

Queenie smiled tightly. "This is nothing but conjecture. You need proof. What's your game plan?"

I tapped the tip of my schnozz. "Sticking my nose everyplace it doesn't belong." My hands waved a ta-da motion, and Queenie crossed her eyes.

Chapter Twenty

If Queenie said, "You must be outta your mind," one more time, I swear, I'd smack her. So far, she'd poo-pooed every one of my ideas, and I was done taking her crap. "The proof isn't gonna jump out and say howdy-do. We need to get into Harvey's office and check it out. I'm telling you. *Something* will point to Harvey."

She said, "Are you crazy?"

Isn't "are you crazy" the same as "you must be outta your mind"? Since I needed her help, I held off smacking her silly for the time being.

Queenie muttered, "What are we? The reincarnation of the Watergate burglars? Hardly a successful caper to emulate. I already told you. Which part of *no* do you not understand? My burgling days are *finito* as in *over*."

I jutted my jaw. "Let me remind you once again. Technically, those do not qualify as burglaries. You were given a key to Ronnie Schwartzman's showroom. And if you remember, most of the times we walked in through an unlocked door."

Queenie flipped her wrist. "Potato, potahto. Tomato, tomahto. We snuck into someone else's empty showroom, uninvited, and went through all his stuff. Was it with his permission? Nope. Is there a better definition of burgling? Nope. And this any different?"

Righteous indignation flavored my tone. "It's our building. We work here. We have every right to be here."

Queenie tsked. "Not in Harvey's office. Not unless he gives his permission." She laughed. "So, Nancy Drew, do you own a skeleton key, or are you planning to break his door down and hope he doesn't notice?"

I rolled my eyes. "Helen sits right outside his office. I bet she keeps a key to his office in her desk drawer. Or we'll get lucky, and Harvey is a trusting guy who doesn't lock his office."

You can set your watch by Harvey Mazer. At his desk at eight on the nose. Lunch from noon to one. Out of the office promptly at five. Not a minute earlier, not a minute later. As predictable as the sun rising in the east and setting in the west. "At least he's long gone. Remember Harvey's mantra? He's only repeated it a bazillion times."

Queenie blanched. "Good God, yes. No doubt, he says it in his sleep. *If you are unable to get your job done from eight to five, you're not doing your job right.* The security guard any problem?"

I waved off the concern. "Nah, he doesn't come on duty until the cleaning crew is finished." I checked my watch. We had an hour. Easy-peasy. Right? What could possibly go wrong?

Queenie twirled her fingers in a circular motion on the sides of her head. "I'm wrong. You're not the crazy one. I'm the one outta my mind for letting you talk me into this." Queenie shivered. "If we get caught, we're gonna get fired."

I grinned. "So, let's not get caught."

****

Harvey's office is the last one on the left side of the executive suite. Helen's desk is set in an open-sided cubicle and stands like a sentry in front of Harvey's door.

I took hold of his doorknob and twisted. Crap, nothing doing. Guess Harvey Mazer isn't a trusting soul after all. Dang.

I sat in Helen's chair. "Stick your head out in the aisle while I go through Helen's desk. If you see Alphonso coming, head him off."

"How?"

I rolled my eyes. "I dunno. Get creative. Smile and say buenos noches. Raise your voice to tell me he's close. You're smart, something will come to you. Don't let him see me going through Helen's desk, or we're screwed before we start."

Queenie said, "I can't speak Spanish. I took German."

I gritted my teeth. "Bat your flirty eyes and say hello, for crying out loud."

I pulled open Helen's center drawer. A pack of sugar-free gum, three mints, two lipsticks, four quarters, a plastic Tampax holder, a box of paper clips, and a mechanical pencil. A small key lay hidden under the pack of gum, but it locked Helen's drawer. No key to Harvey's office. I checked the other two drawers. A bunch of files and office supplies, but no keys. The only things on Helen's desk were a computer and one of those spinning carousels next to her phone. Pens, pencils, highlighters, a metal nail file, the usual, but no key. I wasn't ready to throw in the towel, but if an epiphany didn't come pretty quickly, mark us seriously screwed. I closed the drawer and sighed. "Helen's desk is a big nothing burger."

The intensity of relief in Queenie's voice was pathetically funny. "Ok, too bad. We tried." She grabbed my arm and yanked me out of Helen's chair. "Let's go.

I'm famished. Wanna meet me at Coast Pizza Parlor and share a pie and a salad?"

I jerked my arm free. "Not so fast. I've got an idea."

She screwed her face into a frown. "Crap. Already I'm not in love with the sound of it."

I cuffed her shoulder. "Oh, come on. Where's your sense of adventure?"

She tsked. "I left it at home with my common sense."

As I turned to answer Miss Smarty Pants, the janitor pushed a large trash bin out of the first office three doors from Harvey's. I pointed at the hall and smiled evilly. Queenie sighed with resignation. I waved at the janitor's backside. "See? Ask, and ye shall receive. Our escort into the inner sanctum is walking to us right on time." She stared blankly at me, so I gave her a not-so-gentle shove urging her to move her tush. "Come on. Chop, chop. Hustle your bustle, sister."

Like an obedient duckling, she followed me behind the janitor. As we crept along doing our imitation of Inspector Clousseau in a cleaning crew conga line, I hummed the Pink Panther movie theme song in my head.

The janitor's attention was off to someplace in outer space, and he never realized he had company. So far, he hadn't turned around. I waved Queenie off to fall back. As I tiptoed on the carpet, my pal, the cluck-cluck de grande, cowered behind a large artificial palm tree. Cripes. Go figure. One *minor* fiasco, and she's morphed into a gold-medal champion wimp.

The janitor stopped at the office two doors before Harvey's. I waited until he took the keyring off his work belt. I stepped around in front of him and scared the crap out of the poor guy. He clutched his hand to his heart as

I beamed my most engaging smile. "Hola, Alphonso! buenos noches." I made a big production of wiping my hand across my forehead. "Boy, I am so glad to see you. Listen, I left a very important computer report in Harvey's office this morning. He's already gone home, and the information I need to write a report for him due by early tomorrow morning is on the document. So, please let me in his office so I can get the report."

Alphonso gave me a wary glance and surveyed the hall. "Gee, Seenor Harvey, he not be hoppy I let you een."

I stuck my lower lip out and pouted. "Come on, Alphonso, you don't want me to get in trouble with Harvey, do you?"

Trying to be helpful and still not get himself fired, Alphonso brightened. "Let me go een an get eet for jou. Tell me where eet es an I weel bring eet out."

I flashed him my brightest megawatt smile. "It's nice of you to offer, but a ton of computer reports are in that office. You'd never be able to tell them apart. I'll find it quickly and lock the office. Believe me, he'll never guess you let me in."

I shamelessly batted my eyelashes and gave him my best damsel in distress plea. My voice caught. "Please? It's extremely important." Everything else I said? A big pile of hooey, but not this. Nothing could be more important. David's freedom might depend on it.

Alphonso sighed, "Hokay, but pleeze don't be too long."

I gave him a big hug, and the flush of embarrassment blemished his skin a rosy pink from his neck to his scalp. "Muchas gracias. Alphonso, you're a lifesaver." I crossed my fingers behind my back. "I promise I'll be in and out in a flash."

He opened Harvey's door and went back to the office two down from Harvey's. I waited until Alphonso wheeled his trash bin and cleaning cart into the office. He shut the door, and I waved to Chicken Little hiding behind the tree the all-clear sign.

I said, "You take the file cabinets, and I'll tackle the desk."

Queenie asked, "Are we looking for something in particular?"

I shook my head no. "Nope, but you'll know it when you see it."

For a short guy, Harvey Mazer's desk was the size of an aircraft carrier. I sat at the huge burnished wooden desk and giggled like a kid playing boss at Daddy's office. The guy was a neat freak. A flat-screen computer and an empty metal three-tier in and out basket were the sole occupants of the desktop. Not a file, not a paperclip, not a pen. Zippo. The desktop was so clean, I could eat off it. I checked the time and got nervous. Alphonso worked fast. "Figure five or six minutes max. The last thing we need is Alfonso to come back and see us rifling the office."

Queenie completed her part in short order. "The file cabinets are a bust. Nothing but financial statements, computer reports, and pie charts out the wazoo. Anything important inside the desk?"

I sighed my frustration. "Nada so far. There's only one drawer left." Dang. I was so sure we'd find a smoking gun.

I leaned down and pulled on the bottom drawer. "Crap, the drawer is locked. This must be the pay dirt." I fished around in the center drawer but found no key. I was desperate and running out of time. With no other tricks up my sleeve, I channeled either a girl scout or MacGyver. Take your pick. I bent a paper clip and jimmied the lock. Impressive for someone normally not too good at thinking on my feet, but, alas, no luck. I gave a quick peek down the hall for Alphonso and went back to Helen's cubicle. I pulled the metal nail file out of the carousel. I stuck the nail file tip into the lock and jiggled it around. My sweaty fingers slipped, and I nicked the edges of the lock. Crap. The lock clicked open, and Queenie and I grinned at one another like a couple of lovesick loons.

I opened the drawer and flipped through the files. Nothing special. If the last file had nothing useful, I'd maxed out of ideas. I opened it and yelped louder than I meant to. "Say hallelujah!" I whispered, "Queenie, come here. I found a file of the correspondence between Harvey and the board." I thumbed through the papers and sighed. "Crap. Never mind. Nothing but a bunch of memos explaining financial statements and some meeting notes." My shoulders slumped. "Nothing earthshattering."

She closed the top file cabinet drawer and stood next to me. "Anything else in the file?"

I thumbed through the stack. "One more document in the back." I flipped it open. "It's a letter from Earl Bernard dated right around the time David and Harvey were called on the carpet. Holy guacamole! Read the second paragraph. Earl is telling Harvey that David is out if he doesn't get the profits back to the level before Jack arrived."

Queenie scoffed, "So what? Earl just memorialized in writing everything he said during his phone conversation with Harvey."

I finger-circled the next paragraph. "Keep reading. Paragraph three is legal mumbo jumbo, but according to the next section, David will be fired, and Harvey is gonna be promoted to CEO."

Queenie's finger tapped the tip of her nose. "Huh. That's a completely different scenario from the discussion at the meeting. Whaddya ya make of this?"

I scratched the top of my head. "Say Earl and Harvey made a side deal, and Harvey wanted to move things along. So, he framed David for Jack's murder?"

Queenie dipped her head. "It seems pretty farfetched, but I guess it's possible."

I pointed to the copier in the corner. "Make a copy of the letter, and let's split."

Queenie took the document and turned on the copier on the other side of the office. She groaned, "Geez, this thing is taking forever." She smacked the top of the machine, and it whirred to life. "Finally."

Queenie made the copy and turned off the copier. I re-inserted the letter to the back of the file. I straightened the file back into the order I found it and put it back in the drawer. I pushed the file back, but I couldn't get it to go all the way in. I reached inside to find the obstacle. "Take a gander at this." I held up a mid-size accounting book. Queenie came around and read over my shoulder. I held up the book. "This looks like a ledger for cash sales."

Queenie shrugged, "If it was incriminating, wouldn't the police have taken it when they searched Harvey's office?"

I shook my head. "Not necessarily. Maybe they questioned Harvey about it and were satisfied with his explanation of what it was. If he convinced them that it had nothing to do with Jack, then they didn't see the need to confiscate it." I pointed to the columns. "The dates and figures are in the first two columns, but the transaction names are in some kind of code."

Queenie clucked her tongue. "So? This doesn't prove anything. We don't know the purpose of the ledger. Besides, even if it is for cash sales, they aren't illegal."

I huffed. "They are if you put the cash in your pocket and fail to report it."

Queenie's jaw dropped at the implication. "So, lemme get this straight. Harvey is *skimming money* from the company?"

I gave her the ta-da twirl with my hands. "Why not? He's the CFO. Name a better position in the company to have if you want to steal from it. Say he's stealing and David found out?"

Queenie smirked. "If Harvey is stealing and David found out, you can bet your boat that our vaunted leader stepped right up to demand a piece of the action."

No kidding. No one ever confuses David Workman with honest Abe. "Say Harvey denies he's stealing and buys himself some time to cover his tracks. But after giving his situation some thought, Harvey sees the opportunity to solve all his problems. He kills Jack and frames David for the murder. Harvey eliminates his two problems, and according to the memo from Earl Bernard, Harvey gets David's job. Enough motive for you now, kiddo?"

Queenie wagged her index finger back and forth. "Not until we figure out the code. It may be legit. It could be a shorthand Harvey uses."

I cocked a brow. "And he keeps this *legitimate* ledger hidden in the back of a locked desk drawer? Come on."

Queenie blew out a breath of frustration. "Ok, you win." She wrung her hands. "I dunno, he doesn't seem the type. But if the code isn't broken, the question of whether he's a thief or not remains a mystery." Queenie glanced nervously at the wall clock. "Crap! There's no time left to figure it out. Come on! We've taken too long. Alphonso's a fast worker. He must be finished in the other office by now. He opens Harvey's door, and we're toast. Let's get out while the getting is good."

I jutted my jaw. "We've come this far. We're not leaving without it."

She squeaked as loud as a new pair of patent-leather shoes. "*Are you nuts*? Won't Harvey notice his drawer broken into and the ledger gone?"

Reluctantly, I agreed. "Ok, you stand guard while I make a copy of it. If you see Alfonso, turn out the lights, close the door and get your tush far from the office. I'll hide in the closet and get out later." I put the ledger into the top of the copier and muttered, "Please God, let us not run out of paper."

She said, "Put the face of the ledger flat and set copier for double-page copying. It'll go faster and use less paper."

I gave her a blank look. She might as well be speaking Swedish. Mechanically inclined, I'm not.

She took the ledger out of my hand and snapped. "Good grief. Gimme the ledger and move over. By the time you figure it out, Alphonso will be *done cleaning this* office. You watch the door, and let me do the copies."

Queenie drummed her fingers impatiently while the copier took its sweet time turning on. My heart skipped a beat as Queenie smacked the top of the machine loudly enough for the janitor to hear. "Come on already! Jeez Louise. This is the slowest copier on the planet." As though she'd frightened it into starting, the copier whirred to life again. "Finally."

I almost wet myself as Alfonso wheeled his paraphernalia out of the office next to Harvey's and locked the door. My heart seized as he pulled them towards Harvey's office. I whisper-shouted, hoping she heard me above the whir of the machine. "Hurry! He's coming."

Horizontal prison stripes on someone my height…the vision tied my stomach into square knots. Merde. And imagine my explaining jail to my mother? Yikes. I sagged with relief as Alfonso stopped, shook his head, and turned around. He rolled the equipment cart to the side of the hall and pushed the trash bin back to the office he'd locked. He keyed the door open and pushed the trash bin back into the office, and closed the door behind him. Being a good cavalry scout, I whispered my revised report. "Alphonso forgot something. He went back in, but I'm sure he'll be right out." Queenie's back was to me. I chanced it and said a lot louder, "For crying out loud, finish already!"

Queenie turned her head and talked through gritted teeth. "Give me a break. This is not the fastest copier on the planet, and I am doing it manually." The copier spat out the last page. She handed it to me, and my heart resumed beating normally. Queenie turned off the copier, and it took forever to power off. Hopefully, Alphonso doesn't dust the machine as part of his cleaning routine. Queenie started for the door. "Ok, this is the last one. Let's go."

I stood in front of the door to block her. "Not so fast. We're not leaving until everything is back exactly as we found it. Alphonso has the eyes of an eagle. He'll see we've rifled the office, and it'll bite us in the ass. Keep an eye out. If he comes out, kill the lights, and we'll hide in the closet."

I returned the ledger to the back of the desk drawer under the folder and clicked the lock. I grimaced at the nicks the nail file made. Hopefully, Harvey doesn't notice. Queenie grabbed the copied pages off the desk and shoved them inside her shirt. She gave one last look around, turned off the lights, locked the office door, and put the nail file back in Helen's carousel. We still needed to get past Alphonso. I stole a peek around Helen's desk. Alphonso bent to grab something from the cart and turned his back to us. I gave Queenie the high sign. Now or never. We wriggled as low as two snakes around Alphonso's cart and tiptoed to Queenie's office and locked the door.

We spent the next two hours dissecting the pages and making notes. To go faster, we split the pages in half. Halfway through mine, I noticed a page missing. "I'm missing page number seven. I've got two page sixes and go from page six to eight."

Queenie paged through the documents. "Sorry, not in my stack either. I was in a hurry. My bad. Guess I left one page off. Hopefully, page seven isn't the most important one."

I mused. "No way to do anything about it. And besides, right now, it doesn't matter. If we ever decipher the code, maybe it'll be enough information from pages six and eight to figure out page seven."

I glanced at the clock, surprised at the late hour. Ten o'clock. No wonder my stomach went from growling to howling. Fortunately, I'd given my dock neighbor Muriel Lobowsky a key to my boat. I called her when I realized I'd be late and asked if she'd feed and walk Siggie. My head pounded with a monster headache. My lower back cramped tight as an accordion, and double numbers danced on the ledger columns in front of my eyes.

Two hours at it, and we still couldn't make head or tail of the numbers. We might as well use the purloined papers to line Queenie's kitchen cabinet shelves. This stuff seemed pretty hinky and gave Harvey plenty of motive, but it was certainly no smoking gun. He had the opportunity, but what about the means? Only one way to find out. Get into Harvey's garage to see if he had any rat poison. No biggie. Should be a piece of cake. Wait until I give the good news to Queenie. She will be ecstatic. This ought to be a barrel of laughs.

Chapter Twenty-One

I said, "Pie Charts."

Queenie parroted. "Pie charts."

I grinned. "Yep, pie charts."

She groused. "Ok, I get it. Pie charts. And?"

I'd given Queenie the good news about Harvey's garage. "Yeah, pie charts. Pie charts are our ticket to get into Harvey's garage."

The intensity of her glare could crack a mirror. "I'm not even gonna attempt to figure this one out on my own. So, enlighten me."

I pointed an accusatory finger and aimed it like a gun. "Since you won't help me burgle Harvey's garage, we've got to be invited in."

"And?"

"And we're gonna ask for a tutorial on pie charts."

Her screech hit an octave never reached by a human voice before. "At his *house*? You've gone around the bend this time for sure. Isn't he gonna wonder why we'd ask to do it at his home and not at the office?"

I flicked my wrist. "No problem. Embarrassment. We don't want any of the other executives to realize we're the two dumbest ones in the company."

My brilliant solution earned me an industrial-strength eye roll. "We tell him such a ridiculous pile of hooey, and we *will be* the two dumbest ones in the company. Come on. That's not gonna work. He'll suspect something, especially if it's the two of us." She flashed a hopeful smile. "You're better off trying to pull it off alone."

I shook my head. "Nope. For my plan to work, it has to be the two of us."

She spoke through clenched teeth. "There must be another way."

I shook my head. "Afraid not, kiddo."

She gave me the stink eye.

I waved and gave her the floor. "I'm open to suggestions."

Her shoulders slumped.

I cupped a hand behind my ear. "A little louder, please."

She sighed with resignation. "Let's hear the game plan for this disaster in the making."

I laid it out quickly before she changed her mind.

When I finished, she laughed despite herself. "It's dumb enough to work." She shivered. "It better, or we'll either be in the unemployment line or in a cell next to David."

****

Harvey Mazer lived in an exquisite Modern Tudor-style home on a corner lot with a panoramic ocean view a few steps from the sand on a finger-shaped street in Playa del Rey. But noisy beachgoers and the limited by-permit-only street parking also made part of the package. LAX spanned a mere four miles south, and Harvey's house sat smack in the middle of a take-off flight pattern. Of course, everything worth having, including Harvey's oceanfront paradise, comes with a price.

I turned my vintage '65 bubblegum pink convertible onto Argonaut Street. "You surprised at Harvey's reaction to our request?"

Queenie raised her eyebrows to her hairline. "Stunned. I figured he'd laugh us out of the factory. I guess bean counters don't get many chances to strut their stuff without a gun held to the audience's heads." She pointed to the No Parking signs on both sides of the street. "No wonder Harvey told you to pull into his driveway."

I said, "He has one heck of a view, but..." The rest of my sentence was obliterated by the screech of a 747 taking off. The plane flew directly over our heads, and we two idiots instinctively ducked. I yelled at the top of my lungs. "Imagine living with such a constant racket? You couldn't pay me to move here. I'd go outta my mind."

Harvey instructed us to park in the driveway, go through the open garage, and turn right at the lanai. Two full-size luxury sedans, one black, the other white, sat closely side by side in the narrow garage. Floor-to-ceiling shelves with cartons packed tight as sardines adorned the garage walls. A washer and dryer sat at the back. A metal workbench took up the space in the right rear corner adjacent to the back door. A partially completed wooden birdhouse sat in the middle of the workbench. Whoda thunk? Bean counter-intense Harvey Mazer doesn't exactly come across as a laid-back hobby guy.

Queenie stared at the shelves jam-packed to the ceiling. "Good grief. There are so many shelves. And all of them are filled to the rafters. You're never gonna get through all this crap in such a short time."

I gave the garage a perusal. "There's a lot of stuff, but it's all labeled."

Queenie giggled. "You better be a speed reader."

I favored her with the middle finger salute.

We walked out of the garage, and our jaws dropped. The spacious lattice-trimmed lanai faced west to a gorgeous ocean view. The lanai featured a shuffleboard court and a ping pong table across from a fire pit surrounded by expensive rattan patio furniture. A built-in grill on a brick base in the corner was next to an outdoor wrought-iron dining set large enough to seat a baseball team. Considering its location practically on the sand, Harvey's beach house sat on a huge lot. From the lanai, the yard was terraced down via a flagstone staircase to a free-form figure-eight-shaped pool with a built-in spa surrounded by chaise lounges, a table, and canvas-backed chairs under an umbrella in the corner.

If all CFOs live this luxurious a lifestyle, I wish I'd majored in finance. "Any idea the kind of money a CFO makes?"

Queenie whispered. "Dunno. Either a mint, or you're right. He's skimming money."

Harvey met us at the entrance to the lanai wearing deck shoes, khaki Bermuda shorts, and an untucked Aloha shirt in a Hawaiian print reminiscent of the languishing GOOFYFOOT swimwear line. Cripes.

I'm not so good at controlling my tongue. The words sorta slipped out of my mouth before my brain stopped them. "Harvey, you've got sexy legs!"

Harvey blushed a cute shade of red from his neck to the top of his bald head. He opened the gate to the lanai and laughed. "Why the big surprise?"

I grinned. "I always figured you were born in a tailored three-piece suit."

Harvey slapped his thigh and laughed out loud.

Harvey motioned us in, and we settled into cushioned wrought-iron chairs around the fire pit. A hostess cart held a pitcher, and three glasses stood to the side. Harvey said, "Help yourselves to some lemonade." He smiled his apology. "Ordinarily, it's cocktail time. My wife Goldie and I toast the sunset each evening, accompanied by classical music and a pitcher of margaritas. But since this is a tutorial, if you got snockered, you won't learn anything."

The three of us stared at one another for several awkward moments until I addressed the elephant sitting in the next chair. "Have you seen David? Harriet said she tried to, but the police refused to let her."

Harvey shook his head. "No. I told Harriet not to bother going. The police follow an iron-clad regulation of only prisoners' lawyers are allowed, but she insisted on trying."

Queenie said, "Do you speak to his lawyer? Is David ok?"

Harvey smiled. "Yes. The lawyer and I speak briefly every day. David is doing ok, all things considered. I asked about David being released, but the attorney refused to answer any questions regarding his case."

I gulped. "And if it's a long time? Who's going to run the company?"

Harvey said, "The board appointed me CEO."

Cripes, the body's not even cold, and they've already replaced him.

Harvey Mazer doesn't miss much. He caught our stunned expression and corrected himself. "*Temporary* CEO until David is back."

Pulling a bandage off an open wound would be less painful, but I still asked the question. "And if he doesn't come back?"

Harvey shrugged. "Dunno. We'll jump off the bridge if we get to it."

A shiver passed through me as the cold onshore wind gusted. It was from the wind, right?

Harvey tapped his wristwatch and opened a thick folder. "It's getting late, so shall we get started?"

Before we replied, another jet screamed its departure. Queenie and I ducked under the table, and Harvey burst out laughing. Despite the noise, he spoke in a conversational tone. "Relax. It only sounds as if the plane's gonna land on your head." He grinned. "Eventually, you get so used to the noise, you don't even hear them."

Yeah, right. How about some great beachfront property in Arizona?

Queenie and I took notes as Harvey lectured. News bulletin: Pie charts aren't any more riveting at the ocean than they are downtown. I managed to rouse myself from my stupor and gauged the time. Half through the snore-fest at the sea, I smacked my forehead. "Harvey, I'm sorry, but I need to go out to my car. I've got a list of questions for the pie charts you gave out at the last meeting before David...before the meeting ended. I left my messenger bag in the trunk. Lemme go get it."

I sprinted from the lanai to the garage. I pulled the messenger bag out of the trunk of the convertible and went back into the short, narrow garage.

The two full-sized cars barely fit inside it and left precious little maneuvering room. Three rows of packed shelves covered each wall. Absent an incredible stroke of luck, if Harvey hid rat poison in one of the cartons, in this short a time, I'd never find the needle in a haystack.

I'd been at it a few minutes, but it seemed several days. I'd skimmed two of the three shelved walls and peeked inside a few cartons with potentially promising labels. Regrettably, it was all for naught. I was now intimately familiar with the personal lives of the Mazer family but found no rat poison.

The back wall housed the washer and dryer and was across from the workbench next to a three-tiered steel shelf. The top shelf held cut lumber. Three heavy tool chests, an electric drill, and several types of saws were on the middle shelf.

The bottom shelf was packed with a huge selection of containers. I crouched for a closer examination. Liquid detergents, bleach, and fabric softeners on the side closest to the washer. Next, paints, shellacs, wood stains, resins, paintbrushes, and hidden behind the turpentine and paint thinner, sat two large containers of rat poison.

I opened the photo app on my phone and started shooting. I almost peed myself when Harvey suddenly snuck up behind me and snarked, "Are you generally this nosy, or are you interested in something particular?"

Chapter Twenty-Two

Queenie rolled her eyes. "So, Harvey *actually bought* your cock and bull story?"

I jutted my jaw. "I'm still employed and not sitting in the cell next to David. So, yeah."

She made a sour face. "Tell me again?"

I gritted my teeth. "As I finished taking some photos of the rat poison in Harvey's garage, he comes into the garage and asks why it takes ten minutes to fetch a messenger bag? I'm holding my keys, so I said I dropped my keychain on the way back and used the flashlight app on my phone to search for it on the garage floor. I bent to shine the light under his workbench and inadvertently hit the camera app, and the flash went off."

Queenie snorted. "There's enough baloney in that story to make a sandwich. You whistled past the cemetery this time. You're lucky Harvey's a trusting soul. Anyone else demands to see the photo."

I sniffed with righteous indignation. "I whistled past no place. I came up with a good story, and he bought it."

Queenie shook her head and asked, "Ok, Paulette Bunyon, teller of tall tales. Your next step is…?"

"My next step is I go to see AJ. I lay everything out, and hopefully, she sees Harvey as a viable suspect."

Queenie sighed. "In your heart of hearts, do you really believe Harvey Mazer is capable of *murder*?"

I fired back. "And David is?"

Queenie sighed. "Yeah, he is." The sadness in her voice broke my heart, but not my resolve to get to the truth, no matter what it turned out to be.

****

LAPD homicide detective Akira Jane, "AJ" Yakamura, and her husband Buster Schumansky live in Santa Monica five blocks from the beach in a restored 1920s bungalow. I rapped the brass knocker on their front door. "It's open," AJ's disembodied voice called out from the backyard.

Siggie and I walked through the tidy, southwest-themed house and into the backyard from the kitchen door. Peso, their enormous King German Shepherd, ran at full steam to greet us. Thank goodness he's a lover, not a killer. I planted my feet and braced myself. No one escapes this dog. A speeding freight train is easier to stop. He skidded to a stop and put his baseball-mitt-sized front paws on my shoulders. He grinned and swiped his big tongue across my face and planted a slobbery doggie kiss. Back on all fours, he stuck his long, wet snoot in the rear pocket of my jeans and fished out the Milk Bone I'd hidden. I gave one to Siggie, and the dogs devoured the biscuits in two bites. After sniffing one another for good measure, they chased each other around the yard in a lively game of canine tag.

Decked out in LAPD bike shorts and a T-shirt, AJ had donned a *please do kiss the chef* apron and matching toque to complete her cooking ensemble. The dogs sniffed around the barbecue when AJ glazed a mouthwateringly fragrant Asian-style sauce onto the steaks. AJ gave Siggie a hug and Peso a love scratch behind his ears and pointed the barbecue fork at Peso. "Thanks to you, he picks everyone's pocket. Great for a cop's reputation, huh?"

I took a deep bow. "I live to serve." I uncorked the bottle of Merlot I brought as my contribution to the meal and poured two glasses. "Is Buster getting home soon?" My empty tummy growled loudly.

AJ said, "He's not coming home. He's on the road in the central valley. He'll be seeing accounts in all the small towns off Route 99 and working his way up to Fresno. He'll be gone all week, so it's only us girls." AJ took a sip of wine and smiled. "Nice you invited yourself for dinner. I'm glad for the company but"—she cocked a brow—"besides a freebie meal, why are you gracing me with your presence on a school night?"

I groused. "You've got a mighty suspicious mind."

She laughed. "I'm a cop. They pay me to be suspicious."

I knocked back a fortifying glug of alcoholic-infused courage. "I've got some information."

She narrowed her eyes. "Information?"

I clarified the statement. "Yeah. Information regarding *Jack Tyne's* murder."

AJ struck her cop pose. And an invisible shield covered her face like a curtain coming down at the end of a play. "I never discuss the details of an ongoing case."

I threw up my hands. "You arrested the wrong guy." A picture of Mo Mac's face floated across my memory. I dipped my head. "It's happened before."

AJ's eyes went dark and dangerous. "Not this time."

Mike Schlivnik salesmanship lesson 101: If the front door is locked, climb through the window. "Ok, try this. If you're so sure you're right, let me make a fool of myself."

She laughed out loud and nailed me with my own

words. "It's happened before." She waved the barbecue fork like a magic wand. "Ok, just for the heck of it, and to shut you up, I'll bite. Take your best shot and lay it on me."

Before she changed her mind, I fanned the documents from Harvey's office on the redwood picnic table and opened the photos app on my phone.

She shoved a wad of gum into her kisser and blew a bubble the size of a fist. She glanced at the items on the table. "And all this is…?"

I shrugged. "I'm not exactly sure."

Annoyance tinged her tone. "Then why are you wasting my time?"

I needed her help. So, I bit back a snarky retort sitting on the tip of my tongue and shoved the first ledger page under her nose. "These are pages from a ledger kept by Harvey Mazer. It's a record of cash sales."

AJ rolled her eyes. "This is yesterday's news. We found this in Mr. Mazer's desk drawer and questioned him about it. It has nothing to do with Mr. Tyne's murder."

I ignored her and continued. "The transaction dates are in the first column, the amounts are in the second. The third column lists who made the transaction, but it's in code and we haven't broken the code yet."

AJ sighed. "So much is wrong with this, it boggles the mind. Even if you cracked the so-called codes, why do I care? Cash sales aren't illegal unless you don't report them. I'm a homicide cop, not the IRS, so if they're legal or not, it doesn't do me any never mind. Second, I'm assuming Mr. Mazer didn't give these to you." AJ held her palms out. "Do. Not. Tell. Me. How. You. Got. These. And if, by some quirk of fate, you managed to get them legally, why do you think they exonerate Mr. Workman and implicate Mr. Mazer?"

I detailed the theory I'd laid out for Queenie, but AJ showed zero interest. "None of it is even worth half of a hill of beans. If Mr. Mazer is skimming money, report him to the board of directors, not me. He's a thief, not a murderer."

Undaunted, I kept going. Persistence is my middle name. "Ok, listen to this." I read her the letter from the board to Harvey. She listened but gave me a who-freaking-cares flick of her wrist.

Exasperation punctuated my words as I spelled things out for her. "Here's my take. Harvey sees the chance to get himself elevated to the CEO position if David is fired. Harvey was against Jack being brought on board in the first place. David hired Jack all on his own. Jack made a royal mess of everything and put Harvey's job in jeopardy. Harvey is desperate to get rid of Jack and avoid getting fired himself. David is too, but David didn't get the job done fast enough to suit either Harvey or the board. So, Harvey moves the process along to ensure he gets David's job. He poisons Jack, frames David, and is rewarded by a huge promotion to boot."

I opened the photos of rat poison in Harvey's garage. "Harvey lives at the beach. I took these pictures in his garage. David and Jack met for coffee in David's office every morning. Say Harvey brings the rat poison from home and gets to the office before David and Jack. Harvey laces Jack's coffee every morning, then pours the poison into David's car soap container and hides it."

AJ rubbed her chin. "Is your theory possible? Yeah, it is. But you've got no proof. So, your theory is nothing more than useless conjecture. We performed a thorough search of every office at your factory, including yours and Mr. Mazer's. In contrast to Mr. Workman's, we found absolutely no physical evidence in Mr. Mazer's office to tie him to Mr. Tyne's murder."

AJ waved the barbecue fork around the backyard. "I live at the beach. Rat poison is in my garage." She smirked. "Does that mean I poisoned Jack Tyne?" AJ pointed the barbecue fork at me and issued a stern warning. "Keep your nose out of my investigation. Obstruction is a serious crime. Friend or no friend, I won't allow you to muck up my case with your constant interference. Continue, and I promise you will suffer the consequences."

Friendship be damned, no one threatens Holly Schlivnik. Not even a badge-flashing friend packing a big-ass gun. "Should I take this as a threat, detective?"

The detective huffed. "Take it any way you wish."

Hoping to deescalate the tense standoff, AJ grinned and pointed the fork at the grill. "But for right now, do you wish your steak still mooing as usual, or shall I cook it more well-done?" The sizzling steaks sent out a mouth-wateringly delicious aroma, but I'd lost my appetite.

****

Siggie and I said our goodbyes after an uncomfortably awkward dinner. I dropped the top on the convertible, buckled us both in, and tied the plaid designer scarf around his neck that my style-conscious pooch had absconded with from my collection. I adjusted Siggie's goggles, so his sensitive eyes wouldn't tear, and we headed home.

I took a detour off a jammed Lincoln Boulevard by turning west on Rose Avenue and south on Main Street towards the marina. Siggie aimed his head into the wind, his ears flapping in the cool sea breeze and his tongue lolling from side to side. My pooch is a regular nature boy. I tapped his haunch, and he turned his massive head and gave me an annoyed look as if to say, "Hey, can't you see I'm busy?"

I ignored it and said, "If AJ arrested the right person, I would not need to keep sticking my nose in her case. Your buddy Peso's mommy must be blind as a bat if she doesn't see Harvey as the killer. Do you think she is right?"

"Woof."

The wind gusted. Maybe he didn't hear me right? I repeated the question. "No, really. You don't think it's Harvey either?"

"Woof."

I gave Siggie the stink eye. "Are you just saying it to shut me up so I'll leave you alone, or is it what you really think?"

"WOOF, WOOF!" Sigmund Freud Schlivnik might not talk, but he gets his point across.

I tried a different approach. "Ok. For giggles and squeaks, let's say you and AJ are right. If it isn't Harvey, and you and I are pretty sure it's not David, Carrie is the last suspect left. You agree, right?"

Siggie rolled his hound-dog brown eyes and gave me a look of pity. "Woof."

I clucked my tongue. "Fine, be that way. Remember, from day one, Carrie's always been my favorite suspect."

Siggie dipped his head and gave me the big eyes.

I soldiered on. "So, if we're gonna prove it, we've got to snoop around her house."

Siggie blinked and said, "Woof."

I gave my big boy a love scratch under his chin. "Marvelous. Glad we're on the same page." By the time we boarded the houseboat, Siggie and I had come up with a plan. It might not be the best one, but it was a plan, nonetheless. Selling it to Queenie? Oye. Another story. This ought to be a fun party. Shudder. Gulp. Too bad Siggie can't give her the good news. She'd take it better from him. She prefers his company more.

AJ's threats shook me to the core. All I wanted? To get into bed, pull the covers over my head, and pretend the evening never happened.

As soon as we boarded the houseboat, my cellphone rang. AJ calling to apologize? Or better yet, she had a change of heart? As if. Caller ID said Miguel Martinez. With no hello or how are you, the unhappy camper barked, "It was my understanding you agreed to sell swimsuits and let my detectives solve the crimes."

Good grief. AJ must have called Miguel as we pulled out of her driveway. AJ and Miguel were in the same class at the police academy. Although they were assigned to different precincts when they graduated, they'd stayed in contact. When Miguel got promoted to captain, he requested AJ be transferred to his larger precinct. The higher-profile cases she'd catch in his division put her on the fast track to a promotion of her own. Now, he's her protector as well as her boss. Geesh.

Freaking Fabulous. I needed another lecture like I needed a root canal. I snapped, "If your detectives detected better and arrested the right suspect in the first place, I wouldn't need to get involved."

He spat the words out like he would a rotten piece of fruit. "You're gonna get yourself killed one of these times. You seem to forget...." His voice softened to a sigh. "What will it take to make you understand the concept: Dead is forever?"

I fired back. "Life isn't worth living if you don't stand up for something worth fighting for. If *you* can't understand *that* concept, well, all I can say is, you can't lose what you never had."

Chapter Twenty-Three

I'd almost finished organizing another Bullseye Stores presentation when Harvey's secretary called. Helen's scratchy voice sounded as if she'd gargled using rusty nails. She rasped, "Harvey needs to see you right now. Please come to his office."

I knocked once and walked into Harvey's open office. "You wanted to see me?"

He skipped the pleasantries and growled, "Close the door and take a seat."

My stomach clenched, and I tried to stay calm.

He smiled, but his smile never made it to his eyes. "So, is your report ready to submit?"

I smiled back, but the flush rising from my neck betrayed me. "Which report? I'm working on several."

Harvey spoke with a conversational tone. "The report you told Alphonso you needed to write. You said you left a computer report in my office and needed it to complete the report." Harvey glared. "*That* report."

He steepled his perfectly manicured, stubby fingers under his chin. "It's been crazy since David's arrest. I'm having trouble remembering *which meeting* in my office you left the computer report in. Refresh my memory."

My nervous laugh squeaked like a rubber mouse. "You're right. It has been crazy. Off the top of my head, I can't remember either. Sorry." I stood. "If there's nothing else you want to discuss, please excuse me. I've got a Bullseye Store presentation to finish, and it must go out today."

Harvey's cold eyes stared dead as a shark's. "Sit down. This meeting is not adjourned."

He rubbed his chin and mused. "Seems you're quite forgetful these days. The computer report isn't all you left behind in my office." He put the missing page seven of the ledger on the desk and pushed it to me. "You also forgot to take this." He pointed to his copier. "I found it this morning in the back of the copier feeder."

Way to go, Queenster. Who says I'm the mechanically inept one?

The menace of his smile terrified me. "Good thing I found it. I bet you've been going crazy searching for it."

Harvey, you've no idea. I examined the document with the same level of thoroughness as the Magna Carta. I pushed it back across the desk. "Nope, this isn't mine. If you found it in *your* copier, why would you think a bunch of meaningless numbers on a sheet of paper belong to *me*?"

Anger glittered bright as diamonds in Harvey's gray eyes. "You don't need an explanation."

I gave him the big eyes. "Of course, I do."

He dipped his head. "No idea?"

I shrugged no.

He waved a hand. "No worries. Let me help you out." Harvey sneered. "You lied to Alphonso to get into my office. You went through my desk, searching for…what? You jimmied the locked drawer and pulled a ledger out and copied the pages."

I surreptitiously looked around Harvey's office for security cameras. For someone not in the room at the time, he'd done a darned good job of describing everything we'd done. I struggled to keep a poker face. "Why would I?"

Harvey wrinkled his brow. "An excellent question. And one I've racked my brain asking all morning. But I can't figure out a logical answer. So, let's quit crapping around, and you tell me why you're burgling my office and my house."

My tone rose to righteous indignation. "I beg your pardon?"

He scoffed, "I am a lot of things, but stupid isn't one of them. I didn't fall off the turnip truck yesterday morning."

I wrapped my arms across my chest and glared. I'm a seller with lots of practice outstaring pencil pushers. If he thought I'd make it easy for him, he could kiss my grits.

He rolled his eyes. "Ok. If this is the game you want to play, fine by me. Let me spell it out for you. You and your cohort in crime managed to get the crazy idea into your heads I murdered Jack and framed David to take his job."

Cripes, Harvey's fancy Harvard education is worth every penny.

My dad drilled it into my head that when you've got nothing, make trouble. I jutted my jaw. "Prove it."

Harvey leaned his elbows on his desk and glared. "If I could, you'd already be out the door." He sighed. "I guessed wrong about you. Too bad. Turns out, you're far worse than Jack Tyne. At least the miscreant did not make any attempt to hide his true nature. You? Not so much. You're nothing more than self-righteous slime."

I flinched and tried to explain, even though I could come up with no plausible explanation. "Harvey…"

Harvey held out his palm. "Save it. Nothing you have to say is worth my time." He pointed an index finger at me. "Good thing we need you two, or I guarantee, you'd both be gone. I'm watching you, missy. So, listen carefully. You're now on notice. You two are on my radar." I opened my mouth to protest, but he made a shushing wave and pointed to the closed door. "The meeting is now adjourned. Get out of my sight before I fire you on general principle."

Guess this pretty much puts a damper on an invitation for those sunset margaritas any time soon. Dang. Too bad. I do love a good margarita.

****

Sonia asked, "So you guys gonna keep investigating?"

I gave her a strange look. "Why would we stop?"

Queenie arched her back. "Absolutely not. We are definitely, categorically, positively, watch my lips I'm not stuttering, finished. As in please put a fork in the turkey. It's done."

Joan grinned. "Good to see you two are on the same page."

Queenie glared at me. "The same page? We're not even reading the same book."

I tsked. "I can't understand why you are so upset. Who cares if Harvey figured it all out? He even said he couldn't prove a thing. We weren't fired, and we're not gonna get fired. Harvey blew some smoke up our skirts. Big deal. If he was going to fire us, we'd already be gone."

Sonia dipped her head. "Are you willing to risk losing your job?"

I looked Sonia in the eye. "I risked my life for you,

so risking my job is a no-brainer."

Queenie smacked the table. "Don't you even dare to make a comparison like that. If the tables were turned, Sonia would have done the same for you. The only ass *David Workman* is concerned with saving is his *own*. Is a self-serving jerk worth you putting your career on the line for?"

I shrugged. "If you go through life with expectations, you'll always be disappointed. So, I don't have any. I try to do the right thing by others, but I don't expect anyone to do the same for me."

Queenie spat. "It's a good thing. David's a gold medal champ at disappointing anyone expecting him to back their play."

I shot back. "And David is guilty?"

Queenie shook her head. "No. He's innocent. But that's not the point. This isn't your battle to fight."

I squared my shoulders. "Give me a better battle to fight than one to get to the truth. David Workman is a first-class jerk, but he's *our* jerk. But he's no more a murderer than Mo Mac. Harvey may not be the killer either, so the killer is still loose. If it happened to Jack Tyne, it could happen to any of us. No one is safe until the real person who killed Jack is behind bars. Since AJ isn't looking at anyone else but David, somebody must. I guess it's gonna be me."

Neither of us was willing to destroy our relationship over this, so Queenie and I made a tacit agreement to agree to disagree. As far as this investigation is concerned, I was all on my own. Having no one but Siggie to bounce ideas off made it more challenging, but you've gotta play the cards you're dealt.

Chapter Twenty-Four

Queenie and I planned to meet for dinner Monday night at the Jonathan Beachside Café, a trendy restaurant on South Venice Boulevard half a block from the boardwalk. It doesn't matter if it's three in the morning or three in the afternoon. Parking in Venice is going to be a problem. The money's not the issue. It's the principle. I refuse to plunk ten bucks plus a tip to valet park so some pimply-faced high school kid dressed in board shorts and flip flops joyrides my vintage convertible. So, the only other option was to drive around until I found a parking spot on a side street and hoofed it. This time around, it was more of a challenge, since I needed to park on a specific street. I turned onto Sunset Avenue two blocks from the beach, and for once, the parking Goddess smiled at me. I grabbed a spot as a long-haired guy in a beater old van pulled out. I raised the canvas top and fed the hungry meter half a roll of quarters.

A funky coastal neighborhood, Venice Beach is home to an eclectic boardwalk, every type of eccentric, zany, and crazy, an outdoor bodybuilding muscle beach, and colorful vintage cottages. I headed west to a white-trimmed turquoise cottage on the south side of the street two blocks east of the boardwalk. Carrie Le Beau's cottage. I left the office early enough to get Siggie settled at home, still case Carrie's place, and figure out a game plan with thirty minutes to get to the restaurant, two blocks away. Piece of cake.

The sun had set twenty minutes earlier. The cover of darkness made it easier to sneak around. I walked up the stone path and casually peeked inside. Dang. Shutters closed. I walked around the side of the cottage and peered into an un-shuttered window. The house appeared dark as a witch's cauldron. A narrow driveway led to an unattached one-car garage and a postage-stamp-sized backyard. A peek in the garage told the tale. I pulled on the garage door handle but found it locked. I walked back to the side door. I turned the handle, and surprisingly, the door opened. I hit the flashlight app on my phone and waved it around. No car in the garage.

I'd intended to merely case the place, but far be it from me to ignore a gift-wrapped opportunity when it falls into my lap. I turned on the light switch next to the door and went inside. A push lawnmower stood in the far corner. A washer and dryer sat next to the door with an old-fashioned refrigerator on the other side. Next to it were floor-to-ceiling shelves. The top shelves held tools and yard equipment. Girly Carrie never struck me as the "get your hands dirty" type, so her grandfather must have been the do-it-yourselfer in the family. I shined the flashlight on the lower shelves filled with all kinds of containers. Laundry detergent, fabric softener, Unplug It Plumber, WP-20 anti-greaser, and four packages of rat poison. I bent for a closer examination. Good as a Cat rat bait. Bromethalin is the main ingredient. Thallium. Bingo. Bongo. Ding-Ding. Jackpot. We've got a winner, ladies and gentlemen.

Nothing in the garage with the cottage address on it, so proving the rat poison is on Carrie's property won't be easy. A problem for later. I opened the camera app on my phone and snapped some pictures.

For giggles and squeaks, I opened the refrigerator. The small freezer on top housed the food Lynnie had brought to Carrie from her grandma. But the refrigerator? Whoa. Only one item. Cartons and cartons of juice. The same juice as the juice found in Jack's thermos kind of juice. The same kind of juice that was found in Mo Mac's garage refrigerator. I grabbed a carton to be sure. Not the same kind. The *exact* juice. I stuck my head inside the frig and snapped more pictures.

The cock of the gun hammer behind my right ear turned my innards into jelly. The sledgehammer pounding of my pulse roared in my ears.

Carrie snorted. "Do you need a glass, or do you plan to chug it from the container?"

I straightened up, used my toe to nudge the refrigerator door closed, and slid the phone into my jeans front pocket. Cripes. I'm such a moron. I still held the juice container. "Carrie," I said, "let me explain." Even though my mind drew a blank.

She said, "Turn around slowly. Let's hear the explanation before I blow your head off."

I turned around and pointed to the pistol. "Carrie, I'm not armed. You don't need the gun."

She snorted. "Are you kidding? In this neighborhood? Between the druggies and the gangs, a robbery and worse goes down every night someplace in Venice. Everyone in this neighborhood is packing. The light shone from under the garage door, and I figured a robbery. You're lucky I didn't shoot first and ask questions later the way my grandfather taught me."

I pointed a shaky finger at the pistol aimed at my

heart. "I'm not a robber. Please put the gun down."

Carrie clucked her tongue. "Lemme hear your story, and I'll decide. Don't do anything stupid."

Yeah, right. The battleship stupid already set sail.

She poked the gun into my ribs. "Ok, spit it out."

I said, "I'm meeting Queenie at the Jonathan Beachside Café tonight. Paying their steep valet parking fee is out of the question, so I drove around for a spot. I finally found one in front of a cottage a few up from yours going east towards Pacific Avenue. Lynnie told me the street you lived on and the color of your cottage. I peeked in the front window, but your closed shutters kept the place dark. I went around back, twisted the handle of the garage side door open, and went in. You and I parked next to one another in the Mermaid employee parking lot so I'd recognize your car. If your car is inside the garage, this is your cottage. I'd leave you a note to say I'd been by to see how you were doing. Nothing more to it."

She smirked. "Since the car wasn't in the garage, you expected to find me on one of the refrigerator shelves?"

I waited for a few beats to figure out something plausible. The whopper I concocted? One heck of a stretch, even for a brain trust like Carrie. "Nah. I'm curious about the things single people keep in their frig." I grinned. "Either you're one of those health freak juice purgers, or you cut out a mega coupon in the Argonaut's weekly flyer."

Carrie rolled her eyes. "So, now you've examined the contents of my frig. Congratulations. Why are you really here? To rub my nose in it since you got me fired?"

I shook my head. "Carrie, you give me way too much credit." I hiccupped a nervous laugh. "I wasn't consulted before David hired you and Jack, and I certainly wasn't asked for my opinion whether to keep everyone or let Jack's team go."

Carrie snarled. "I don't believe you. You and Lynnie are thick as thieves, and you two got me fired." Carrie's voice caught. "I'll never find another job in the middle of the season."

She was right. No one is hiring. Ironic. Same problem for Lynnie: Too late for the current season but too early for the next one. Turnabout is fair play. "You didn't care if Lynnie found another position." Good grief. If I live through this, I need to learn how to control my tongue.

Carrie looked at the juice container in my hands, and her eyes grew big with recognition. "You're full of it with the *in the neighborhood song and dance*. You're sniffing around to pin Jack's murder on me."

Hmm. She isn't such a dumb blonde after all.

I tsked. "You're being paranoid." I narrowed my eyes. "Or you're guilty." I willed Carrie not to notice the pop sound as I slowly unscrewed the safety top of the juice container. I loosened it enough to flip off, put my thumb on the cap, and waited.

She waved the gun at my jeans. "Give me your cell."

I batted my eyes. "Cell?" I patted the front of my jeans. "I guess I left it in the car."

Carrie snorted. "Get real. I'm blonde, not blind. The one you put in your pocket. Take it out nice and easy and lay it on the ground."

I shook my head. "No."

Her eyes went wobbly. "Give it to me," she screamed. "Or I swear, I'll shoot you dead."

Carrie's high-pitched voice carried. I prayed a nosy

neighbor heard her screeching and called the cops. As if. I'm not so lucky. Besides, God helps those who help themselves. My heart leaped to my throat, but my voice came out remarkably calm. "Don't do something you'll regret. Put the gun down and let me go. We'll pretend this never happened, ok? No harm, no foul."

Her maniacal laugh reminded me of the one at the funhouse at the old Pacific Ocean Park, the long-gone popular amusement park at the foot of the Santa Monica pier.

She growled from the back of her throat. "Nothing doing, sister. I'm not as dumb as you think I am. You took a bunch of photos. You're gonna take them to the cops and say I poisoned Jack." Carrie's voice cracked. "First, you get me fired. Now you accuse me of murder. Why do you hate me? I've never done anything to you." She pointed the gun at my head. "This is the last time I'm gonna say it. Next time, the gun's gonna do my talking, and it won't say it as nicely." She commanded. "Give. Me. The. Cell. Phone. Now."

I lost all sense and taunted her. "You want it?" I waved her on. "Come and get it."

All the anger, fears, and frustration of dashed hopes and shattered dreams festering inside Carrie exploded with the force of a timebomb. She gave a primal scream rising from the depths of her soul. Carrie lunged at me. And it was now or never. I flipped the top off the juice container and aimed for her eyes. She scrubbed her fists into her eyelids, rubbing in the acidy juice in deeper, burning her eyes even more. She staggered around like a blind guy trying to dance. She teetered back and hit her head on the sidewall. She screamed as she fell and dropped the gun. The gun hit the ground and bounced. A wild shot obliterated the juice container and blew the pieces out of my hands. The deafening sound of the shot reverberated around the small, one-car garage as loud as the blastoff of a rocket. I clapped a pair of numb palms over my ears that were now ringing loud as a fire alarm. The gun skittered to the back of the garage, but I didn't stick around to hunt for it. I ran out the side door as if my hair had caught fire. My ears still rang as loudly as Sunday morning church bells as I jumped into the car and peeled rubber, grateful to escape with my life.

Chapter Twenty-Five

AJ invited Siggie for an overnight visit. This was her signal of an uneasy cease-fire of our war of words. After AJ and I shared a takeout pizza, I admonished my pooch to be a good guest and said goodbye. I was more than ready to get home and crawl into bed.

I arrived at the security gate at the same time as my dock neighbor, who juggled an armload of grocery bags while fumbling for her keys. Muriel Lobowsky, the octogenarian sailor extraordinaire, lived aboard the thirty-six-foot ketch at the end of the dock. I keyed the security gate open and waved her in.

Muriel is an independent old coot who sailed solo around the world in her mid-seventies. This is a feisty, independent woman for whom age is merely a number and one who wouldn't cotton to being coddled. I cautiously pointed to the heavy-looking bags. "Muriel, those bags must be awfully heavy. Let me help you."

She smiled a toothy smile and, surprisingly, with no hesitation, shoved two full bags into my arms. This was an unexpected first. I gave her a closer perusal for signs of illness. She rolled her bony shoulders and laughed a gravelly laugh. "I was too lazy to make two trips like I should have, but I overestimated my wingspan capacity. You're a lifesaver." I shifted my messenger bag strap across my chest and let Muriel go ahead of me. We got to the gangplank, and she said, "Oh, before I forget, happy birthday."

I narrowed my eyes. "Muriel, I appreciate the good wishes, but today isn't my birthday. It's on March twenty-sixth. You're a few months shy."

Her frown cut the wrinkles deeper into her weathered face. "March? You sure?"

I laughed. "Yeah, of course, I'm sure. One date I'd never forget is my birthday. What made you think today is my birthday?"

She said, "I opened the security gate earlier this evening to go to the market, and a young woman holding a package stood outside and asked if I knew you. I said yes, and she said today is your birthday, and she wanted to surprise you with a gift. She asked if I'd let her in the gate, and I said sure." Muriel's face clouded. "Gee, I hope I didn't do something wrong letting her in."

It's never a good idea to let strangers onto the dock. But the old gal's face turned so stricken, I let her off the hook. "Nah. I'm sure she got the date wrong or something. Did she happen to say her name?"

"No." Muriel's narrow shoulders sagged. "I should have asked, but honestly, I was in a hurry. I needed to get to the market and didn't give it a no, never mind." She hung her head. "Jeepers, I'm so sorry. A bonehead old lady mistake."

Internally, I agreed but tried to make the old gal feel better. "No worries. Can you describe her?"

Muriel's face brightened. "Oh sure, no problem. I pride myself on paying attention to details." Muriel's hazel eyes lit mischievously. "It's the secret to my staying vertical this long. It was especially dark with no moonlight, but we stood directly under the streetlight. We faced one another, so I got a good look at her. Young gal, in, I'd say her early-to mid-twenties. Five feet fourish. Nice figure, but not too big on top. Expressive light eyes, dark, wavy-curly, mid-length hair, and oh yeah"—Muriel pointed to a spot on her lip—"a small beauty mark right above the left side of her upper lip." Muriel gave me a hopeful smile. "Help any?"

An unwelcome knot formed in the pit of my stomach and twisted my gut into a pretzel. Muriel described Lynnie Stubbs to a T.

Curious. I shook it off. Lynnie is a landlubber, so it made no sense for her to come near the marina. Lynnie Stubbs had been on my boat a few times. The last time, she turned green as a grasshopper and lost her lunch when the boat rocked with the wind. She vowed never to step foot on my yacht again. Smart money says never say never. Say she put her big girl panties on and took Dramamine.

Even so, getting past the wrong birth date? Impossible. She'd never get the date confused. Lynnie shares the same birthday with me.

Muriel interrupted my game of mental ping pong. "So, do you recognize her?"

I said yes, and I'd be sure to give her the correct date of my birth. Muriel's muscles relaxed as I plastered on a fake grin. "It's never too early for a birthday surprise, is it?"

We walked to the end of the gangplank and stopped dead in our tracks. We both took a sniff of the salty air and blanched. Between the marine wildlife and messy marina people, it's not uncommon for the air at the beach to smell bad at times, but this one's a stinker of epic proportions. The stench worsened the closer to my boat we walked. I said, "Hopefully, no one died again."

Muriel gave me the big eyes and squeaked a nervous laugh.

I said, "Don't laugh. It happened a few years ago. The liveaboard guy in the cabin cruiser on the channel-side slip next to mine at the time had died in his sleep. He lived alone, and no one discovered him for a week until everyone in the basin complained to the dockmaster about the stench."

Muriel twitched her nose. "No question about it now. Something *definitely* died."

I frowned. "I hope it's not our pal the crane. I'd miss saying good morning to him every day." The nosy crane and I shared a storied history. No one gave me a heads-up about the crane. On my first night on the houseboat, the crane came aboard to welcome me to the neighborhood. He stood perched behind me and rested his big head on my shoulder as I keyed the forward door. He stuck his beak next to my ear and cawed as I unlocked the door. By a sheer miracle, I didn't wet my pants or fall in the drink. I screamed my head off and scared the stuffing out of the crane and everyone else on the dock.

"Nah. Not to worry." Muriel grinned. "He's a tough old bird. He'll outlive us all."

We stopped at my dock, and I offered, "Do you want me to carry these to your boat? I'm happy to."

She motioned for me to hand her the bags. "Nah, it's not too far. I'm good." An onshore breeze ruffled Muriel's wavy grayish-white hair. She twitched her nostrils and pinched her lips. "Boy, this is one gnarly odor. I keep the cabin cool when I sleep, so I open my portholes at night." She grimaced. "I hope the stink gets blown out to sea by the time I'm ready for bed, or I won't sleep well with the portholes closed."

I handed her the bags, and we said our goodbyes. I put one foot on the bow and stopped. I'd come close, but so far, never fallen into the drink, so I always checked my footing on the deck. I dropped my messenger bag on the dock and screamed so loud my next-door neighbor Mark, the ex-Navy Seal, ran out onto his deck only clad in his boxers. I kept screaming, and pretty soon, every liveaboard in the basin congregated at my slip, holding their nose. Mark yelled, "Are you hurt?" I shook my head, but the words stuck in my throat. Mark jumped onto my boat and bent his knees for a closer look. He shook his head and said, "Holy crap!"

How I missed stepping on them is a miracle. Some sicko had laid twenty-seven dead rats across the length of my foredeck and used the carcasses to spell out RATS FOR A RAT. I shook like a sapling in a windstorm as Mark wrapped his strong arms around me. My throat throbbed sore from screaming as I cried into Mark's chest. I lifted my head for some air, and the dock started spinning. I pulled myself out of Mark's arms and heaved my Thai chicken pizza over the port side of the boat.

Muriel dropped the groceries at her boat and ran back to my slip. Betty from the sloop two slips from mine yelled she'd already called security. A few minutes later, two LA County Sheriff's squad cars barreled to our basin.

Two of the cops drew their guns and inspected my houseboat from stem to stern. The doors and windows were still locked. Nothing missing or out of place, but the violation still twisted my heart. The cops put crime scene tape around my boat and took zillions of photos. They spread this black filmy powder on my deck and dusted it for fingerprints. Cripes, I'll never get the stuff out. They interviewed everyone on the dock, but with it being a moonless night, no one saw a thing.

The other two officers escorted me to the security office located on the lower level of the first of three apartment buildings bisecting the marina. They kept me for hours and asked the same questions again and again. But I had no answers as to who or why someone would do something so awful.

They finished questioning me at one in the morning. One of the marina's security men escorted me back to the houseboat. I packed a bag and ran out of Dodge. I arrived at Queenie Levine's townhouse in the middle of the night as a cross between an escaped convict and a refugee. She didn't ask for an explanation and I never offered one. I crawled under the covers in Queenie's guest bed and cried my eyes out.

Chapter Twenty-Six

I finished my story and surveyed the table. The Yentas stared at me, dumbstruck.

Joan wrinkled her nose. "Twenty-seven dead rats?"

I shuddered. "Yeah. Laid across my deck and spelled out RATS FOR A RAT."

Hope's jaw dropped. "You stood on the boat and counted them?"

Queenie has two cats, and I'm deathly allergic. Even though she put them in the garage, I still sneezed all night. I was tired, cranky, and scared. I tried to tamp back my annoyance but failed. I snapped with the intensity of a hungry gator. "If I counted the number of rats is the most critical part of the story for you?"

Hope flinched from the rebuff and sniffed. "No, just curious. Sorry."

Sonia wrung her hands. "You've gotta be a real sicko to do such a horrible thing."

Hope's fist flew to her lips. "My God, is it possible Lynnie is responsible?"

I'd tortured myself by asking the same question a million times. It was hard to wrap my head around the possibility, but Muriel's spot-on description of Lynnie Stubbs left little room for doubt. "If I go by the description Muriel gave, no question, it's Lynnie. But it doesn't pass the sniff test. She'd never get my birthday wrong. It's the same date as hers. Besides, I doubt she'd step foot on my boat again. Lynnie is a landlubber, not a sailor. The last time she came aboard, the wind jostled the boat in the slip, and she barely made it to the head before she horked out her lunch."

Sonia logically said, "Maybe she took Dramamine."

Joan wiggled an index finger back and forth. "Nah. Lynnie has no motive. Holly went to bat for her and kept her employed. This is the handiwork of someone Holly pissed off pretty badly."

Queenie snarked. "No shortage of worthy candidates."

I took a few beats before I answered. Carrie Le Beau is my favorite choice. Since our run-in was one of those he said/she said things with no witnesses, I had no proof it actually happened. So, I never told anyone about it. Not even Queenie. I gulped a fortifying swig of coffee and described my nearly fatal adventure.

Joan's judgmental glare could have bent a steel beam. "Lemme get this straight. You sneak into Carrie Le Beau's garage. You sniff around. You find rat poison on a shelf, and a frig packed full of the same kind of juice as in Jack Tyne's thermos. You take some pictures. Carrie sees a light in the garage. Figures she's being robbed. She sees you take the pictures. Confronts you. Aims a gun at your head. She demands you give her your phone. You refuse. She threatens to shoot you. You tell her to come and get it. She does, and you throw juice in her eyes and run outta the garage? I'd hate to be inaccurate. I got all the details correct, didn't I?"

I dipped my head.

Joan crossed her arms across her chest and snapped, "And it never occurred to you to tell someone, I dunno. Your friend, the *cop*? You do understand for an intelligent person, you are an *idiot*, right?"

Joan steamed as powerful as a locomotive. Instead of defending myself and fighting a battle I'd never win, I chose contrition. "No, not until now. When you describe it, ok, some of the moves weren't the smartest."

Joan's husky voice rose a few hundred octaves. "No kidding. Tell me, which part *is* the smart part? I obviously missed it. Sneaking into the garage? Or the part when she waved the gun at your head and you egged her on to take the phone?" Joan glanced around the table. "Come on, girls. Help me out. I'm not seeing it. Which part do you guys think is the smart part?"

So much for contrition getting a sympathetic ear. I turned to the Yentas for some support, but they glugged the rest of their coffees and stayed mum. Gee, girls, thanks a bunch. I appreciate the help.

Lucky me. Joan hadn't finished her tirade. "Nobody else sees it? So, the rest of you are as blind as me."

Sonia said, "The rat thing on the boat and the Carrie run-in must be related, right?"

I squirmed with frustration. "Of course. But since there's no proof, it's going nowhere."

Queenie funneled her lips. "I'd put on my big girl panties and call the *real detective*. This little adventure of yours is out of control. You're in over your head."

I couldn't come up with an argument, but oh boy. This ought to be fun. If your idea of a good time is a trip to the dentist. Cripes.

****

Detective Yakamura shoved a wad of pink gum in her mouth and blew a bubble the size of a fist. She took a copy of the sheriff's report and fluttered it like a fan. "I've spoken to the sheriff's department. Regrettably,

they have no progress to report in identifying the perp."
She gave me an expectant look. "Any guesses?" AJ
waved the report under my nose. "Do you have *any idea*
why someone spelled out *RATS FOR A RAT* by using
dead rodents as letters on your boat?" She folded another
wad of pink gum into her mouth and blew a bubble the
size of a tennis ball.

I squirmed in my seat and observed Siggie and Peso
chasing one another in a circle. I completely related.

AJ's pointy front teeth popped the bubble. "Hey,
remember, you called me, not the reverse. You called for
a reason and not to shoot the breeze. So, spit it out
already."

I squirmed some more and finally told her.
Everything. I finished spilling my guts, and guilt
strangled my heart as if I'd confessed to a crime. I guess
from her perspective, I had. She gave me the big eyes
and blew another bubble, this one the size of a newborn's
head. She popped the bubble and eyed me as if a prize
steer at a cattle auction. Her judgmental silence made me
twitchy.

She quirked a lopsided grin. "Boy, you're a piece of
work."

I twisted my lips into an aw-shucks grin. "Yeah, so
I've been told. Tell me something new. So, detective,
you got a take on this?"

AJ blew another bubble. "You scared Carrie Le
Beau, and she returned the favor..."

"*But?*"

AJ held out her hands. "*But* Carrie Le Beau doesn't
fit the description our witness gave."

I said, "Our witness didn't see Carrie or Lynnie, or
anyone, place the dead rats on my boat. Our witness is

an older woman who described someone who *resembles* Lynnie Stubbs trying to deliver a birthday present to me on the wrong date."

AJ said, "Have you considered they're the same person?"

I kept at it. "Muriel described Lynnie to a T, but it makes no sense. Whoever did such a vicious act of vandalism meant to do me harm. Lynnie isn't a horrible person. She's a gentle soul. She'd never get my birthday wrong. It's the same date as hers. And she wouldn't come within twenty miles of the marina. She became seasick the last time she came on my boat."

AJ gave me one of those are-you-really-so-dumb rolls of her eyes. "Medications do exist for it."

I nodded my agreement. "True, but it doesn't sit right. This isn't something she'd ever do. There must be another explanation. Muriel is in her eighties. Her eyesight isn't as good as it used to be. I dunno, Lynnie Stubbs? I'm having a problem wrapping my arms around her doing something so awful."

AJ smiled with the depth of sadness of those who see awful things every day. "You'd be surprised at the terrible things good people are capable of if they're pushed far enough. I see it every day."

I shook my head. "I get it, but the pieces to this puzzle won't fit together, no matter how I rearrange them. She has no motive. We're on the same team. The timing of this. The meanness of it. Just screams retaliation. It must be Carrie Le Beau. And now what?"

AJ folded her arms across her chest. "*Now* you quit investigating and let me do my job."

I asked, "How?"

AJ grinned. "Shake a few trees and see which fruits fall to the ground."

Chapter Twenty-Seven

I said, "If looks killed, I'd be pushing a bunch of daisies around at the Heavenly Home Cemetery."

Joan said, "So, I take it Lynnie wasn't thrilled to hear from the detective."

I snorted like a hog in heat. "The understatement of the century."

Queenie added her fifty cents. "I'll say. Lynnie's been on a tear for two days. She's the talk of the factory. Everyone is staying as far from her as possible. For a quiet kid, it turns out she has quite a mouth. Bernice, our head patternmaker, made a simple request for additional information, and Lynnie nearly took Bernice's head off. Human resources received so many complaints, Eleanor, in HR called Lynnie in and gave her a warning so strong, it went onto her employment record."

Sonia said, "You said she's a smart kid. Once you explained, she must have understood."

I sighed. "You're assuming she let me explain."

Hope's jaw dropped. "She didn't?"

I shook my head. "No. She had zero interest in hearing my explanation."

Sonia reasoned. "Did your friend the cop accuse her of anything? Threaten to arrest her?"

I scratched my head. "I've seen AJ's aggressive side in action, and it's not pretty. But the heck of it is no, she wasn't. AJ said she asked the standard procedure questions and conducted a normal interview."

Hope asked, "So, why did things go off the rails?"

I rubbed my chin. "It depends on who is telling the story." The Yentas stared at me blankly. "According to AJ, it started as nothing out of the ordinary. She's a go-by-the-book cop. AJ called Lynnie for a meeting, and Lynnie agreed to see her. They set an appointment, and AJ came to Lynnie's office."

Joan said, "And?"

"And two questions in, Lynnie went bonkers."

Joan frowned. "She had no idea someone put rats on your boat?"

"We hadn't discussed it directly, but unless she lived under a rock, she heard what happened. The story's been a hot topic at the factory for the last few days. But I didn't tell her Muriel described her to a T."

Sonia said, "So?"

"So, AJ asked Lynnie if she'd ever been on my houseboat, and Lynnie said yes, one or two times." I quirked a grin. "The boat rocked a little, and Lynnie turned green at the gills. So, I'm having a hard time imagining her doing the deed. She's a landlubber who lives in a mountain canyon. The marina is the last place on the planet she'd come to for anything."

Sonia crossed her arms. "What about an alibi?"

I shook my head. "She lives alone except for the dogs. She fed the pups, heated one of her grandma's care package meals, caught some TV, and called it a night."

Sonia asked, "Dramamine?"

Joan said, "Let's say she took it. Still, her fingerprints are someplace on your houseboat, right?"

I wiggled my digits. "She didn't wear gloves when she came aboard, so, yeah. Her prints must be in the head, the galley, the aft deck, the guard rails."

Hope's hands flew to her cheeks. "No wonder she went crazy. It puts her at the scene of the crime."

I said, "AJ asked her to give a fingerprint sample, and Lynnie told her to pound sand unless she brought a warrant."

Hope made a ta-da motion. "She has something to hide."

Joan asked, "Lynnie have anything to say to you?"

I laughed. "Oh yeah. Plenty. She gave it to me with both barrels. She's pissed I didn't warn her and angry I'd given AJ her name at all. But most of all, she's furious I'd even believe her capable of such a horrible thing. I tried to explain that I didn't, but Muriel's description fit her perfectly and was a major part of her statement to the sheriff. I had no choice but to tell AJ. Lynnie shot back everyone has choices. Including her." I glanced around the table. "If she doesn't get fired, it might be for the best if she quits. If she's not able to get beyond this, I doubt we'll be able to work together. I guess time will tell."

Sonia held out her fingers. "Is the detective getting a warrant for her fingerprints?"

I shook my head no. "Nope. Muriel's description of Lynnie at the boat isn't enough to get a judge to sign it. With no physical evidence tying Lynnie to the crime, the police lack probable cause. Lynnie has no police record. So, even if her fingerprints are on my boat, nothing in the system matches hers."

Joan said, "So Lynnie twisted her knickers in a bunch for nothing?"

The sixty-four-thousand-dollar question. "In my book, yes. I understand getting upset, but her reaction went to a crazy level. Something else sent her over the edge."

Joan tapped her fingers on the table. "Have the police interviewed Carrie?"

I rolled my eyes "Oh yeah. AJ interviewed them both." I pursed my lips. "Carrie denied everything."

Queenie's eyes bugged. "She denied having the gun?"

I smirked. "Nope. She admitted to *owning* a gun. She denied holding the gun on *me*. She denied I'd ever been at her cottage. No gun, no confrontation. Nada. She said the last time she saw me was at Jack's memorial service. AJ showed her the photos I took, and Carrie denied they were of her garage. AJ asked to see the garage and for a fingerprint sample, and Carrie told her the same thing as Lynnie. No warrant, nothing doing."

Joan drew an imaginary line on the table. "So, where does this leave things?"

I bunched my shoulders. "For the moment, no place. If the police can't compare her fingerprints to the ones at the scene, there's no physical evidence tying Carrie to the crime. The probable cause issue is the same for Carrie as Lynnie." My voice shook, but my resolve remained unshaken. "Twenty-seven rats didn't fling themselves onto my boat deck, spell out RATS FOR A RAT, and die. One of these two women is responsible. This is my life someone is trying to ruin. Since AJ nor the sheriff can get to the bottom of this, it's gonna be up to me."

Chapter Twenty-Eight

I tore my office apart looking for a folder holding paperwork required to accompany the samples for another customer's style meeting the day after tomorrow. I searched high and low, but I couldn't find the documents anyplace. I racked my brain. Think. Think. Had I taken them home to work on? No. Not in the customer account book, not on my desk, not in the closet, not in my messenger bag, and not in my briefcase. It took me two days to complete those complicated forms. The presentation shipped early in the morning, so there was no time to redo the forms.

I almost dialed the buyer to ask for an extension when I remembered I'd given a copy of the documents to Lynnie. Hallelujah! We keep copies of every document in customer binders housed in Lynnie's office. I dialed Lynnie's extension but got no answer. I called the design studio and the test lab, but no one picked up at either place. I went across the hall and peered into her still-lit office. "Lynnie," I called, "You still working?" No answer.

I checked my watch. Almost five. Lynnie is one of the first into the office every morning, so she had already left for the day. With things still pretty frosty between us, she didn't bother saying good night. I had no choice. I picked up the handset to dial but quickly put it back in the cradle. If she was in the mountains, she'd have no cell service. Wait until the morning to ask her? And spend a sleepless night obsessing about the darned file? As if. I didn't relish rooting around in her office, but I was out of options and time.

I went into her office, sat at her desk, and checked around. No account folders on her desktop. I opened the center drawer. Nothing but highlighters, pens, pencils, paper clips, a box of staples, four quarters, and a package of gum. The top drawer held a Polaroid camera, packages of film, and laminate paper.

The bottom drawer housed blank production forms, sample request forms, and trim sheet documents. Behind them, shipping forms and a prescription bottle were stashed in the back corner. Huh? My natural nosy parker curiosity peaked, so I took the bottle out. Dang, the patient's name was smudged, and the medication name was unpronounceable. Nor did I have any idea what it was for. So, Lynnie is ill? She'd been acting crazy, but she didn't appear sick. If she's ill, is it serious? Are there strong side effects with the medication that explain her outrageous behavior? I played a mental tennis match inside my head. Should I ask her? If you want the answer, of course, you do. If you don't ask, you don't get. On the other side of the coin, if she wanted me to know, she'd tell me. Should I ask? Of course not. If I did, she'd realize I'd been snooping and invading her privacy. Good grief. This is exactly the way Peso and Siggie are when they're chasing their tails.

Something important niggled in the back of my brain. I closed my eyes to concentrate. Wait a Cincinnati minute. The medication rang a bell. Why? My stomach dropped a few stories. Holy cow. Where had I heard it from? My blood froze. From Lynnie Stubbs. Lynnie said she told AJ she didn't recognize, let alone take the medication. So, why is a vial of it inside her desk? I still needed to find the folder, so I pushed the issue back to the deal-later department and moved on.

The lower-level shelf of the cramped, narrow storage closet held fabric swatches and trims in plastic containers. The middle shelf housed bolts of sample fabrics. Naturally, the top shelf housed all the account binders. I stretched on my tiptoes, but at only four-foot nine inches, I was not even close. I looked around for something to climb on. I bent to get the stepstool on the floor, and a container in the far corner caught my eye. I leaned in to read the label. Rat poison. I smacked my head silly on the shelf when Lynnie said, "Something specific you needed?"

*****

AJ bought Lynnie's recurring rodent problem for having the rat poison story, but not the vial. AJ confiscated it and sent it to the lab for fingerprint testing. Good news/bad news. If AJ gets a warrant for Lynnie's prints and Lynnie's are on the vial, David's off the hook, but Lynnie is toast.

In the dark on so many things, I called the one person who could shine a light. I breathed a sigh of relief when my favorite coroner answered the phone. "This Jack Tyne murder is getting too close to home. First, someone puts dead rats on my boat, and now an AFIB medication bottle is planted inside Lynnie's desk. The two must be connected."

Snip said, "Not necessarily. The vial may be a plant, or a careless Ms. Stubbs failed to dispose of it." Regret hollowed my pal's voice. "You must consider she might not be the good guy she seems to be. Detective

Yakamura made a pretty strong case."

Not the answer I wanted. "Snip," I whined into the phone. "I'm telling ya, Lynnie isn't the perp. There isn't a mean bone in her body. Compare the prints taken from my boat to the ones on the vial from Lynnie's desk. Whoever vandalized my boat planted the vial in Lynnie's office. The connection between the two acts makes sense to me."

Snip said, "The connection may make sense to you, but proving it is another thing. The lab will certainly compare the two sets of fingerprints. But if Ms. Stubbs and Ms. Le Beau aren't in the system and won't volunteer to give their fingerprints, it's going to remain a mystery unless Miguel Martinez is convinced there's enough probable cause to get a warrant."

I said, "The prints from my dock cleats and the vial may match, but they won't belong to Lynnie."

Snip said, "I wouldn't bet the farm on it. It's a bet you may lose."

Crap. I gotta quit dialing Doctor Death's phone number.

Chapter Twenty-Nine

Another long, difficult day. Delivery problems, cranky sales reps, frustrated accounts. I get it. Stores can't sell empty hangers. While the issues were beyond my control, nonetheless, the problems happened on my watch. So, guess who's at the receiving end of all the complaints? That's why they pay me the big bucks. As if. This day I batted a thousand. I made no one happy. Ordinarily, I'm no clock-watcher, but I practically pole-vaulted out of the office the minute it struck five o'clock. I wanted no company. Imitating Greta Garbo, I vant to be alone. I called Muriel from the car and asked her to take Siggie for the night. I love my pooch to pieces, but after this stinker of a day, I didn't have the energy for all the attention he required. Lucky for me, the old gal loved having my dog for company. He was the grandson she never got to spoil. LOL. Color me a happy camper after a takeout pizza, a bottle of Chardonnay, a half-pint of Rocky Road, and some peace and quiet worked their magic.

I took the Marina freeway west until it dead-ended at Lincoln Boulevard. I turned into the homestretch onto Washington Street, and the difference was like night and day. One minute the stars are twinkling their good night to the moon, and the next minute the fog rolls in thick as pea soup, and seeing the car in front of me isn't possible. So much for the takeout pizza. The fog will only get worse the farther west I go. Being out longer than necessary and making extra stops is not a brain surgeon's move. Chardonnay and chef's surprise would be the new special of the evening.

My brain switched to autopilot at Admiralty. I crept into the Porto Paloma Marina subterranean parking structure in one piece by sheer instinct. I climbed the steps to the street level at Palawan Way and couldn't see across to the security gates. The fog rolled in from the ocean in heavy waves and blanketed the ground with a spongy veil. With fog so thick, boats moored a hundred yards from the parking structure disappeared from view. I put an ear out and listened for any engine noises. The eerily quiet marina lay draped by a shawl of goopy fog. No one with a brain is out in this mess. I crossed Palawan Way and counted three basins to the left by memory. I keyed open the security gate at number seventeen hundred and cautiously made my way down the gangplank.

All the fun and games began at the end of the gangplank. No guard rails, no footlights, nothing on the narrow finger of a walk dividing the slips to guide me. Fog creates havoc on depth perception. There were no guideposts to prevent miscalculating the width of the walk and meandering into the drink. My slip is on the west side of the basin, six slips from Muriel's boat at the end of the dock. From the end of the gangplank, mine is the eighth slip to the end. Plenty of opportunities to walk off the dock and into the murky channel water. I used the dock boxes in front of every slip as a guide and counted from the gangplank to the channel to find my houseboat. It was high tide, and the sea had risen to its highest level. As I leaned in to put my messenger bag on the forward deck, I recognized my dog barking. Siggie sensed me home. Poor pooch. I bet he was confused as to why I hadn't come to get him. My heart twisted into knots of guilt at being a bad doggie mommy. Should I fetch my furry fella? I turned towards the end of the dock, but the thick fog had swallowed Muriel's boat. Nah. Better not chance it. I'd get him in the morning. I ignored his continuous barking and stepped over the forward rail.

The leeward wind blew strong. The channel was still at high tide. Pushed by the wind, the boat drifted towards the far side of the slip. I stretched my full length to get aboard. I clasped the guard rail and put my left foot on the top of the deck for balance while I swung my right foot. Mid swing, the boat lurched towards my neighbor Mark's boat. With the fog so thick, it was impossible to see that the forward and aft spring lines had become fouled and loosened by the tide from the cleat hitches. The lines dangled uselessly in the water, and the houseboat floated towards the open end of the slip. My insufficient wingspan prevented me from keeping hold of the guard rail and pulling myself onto the boat. I wrapped my fingers around the forward cleat and tried to hold on.

I teetered half on, half off while the houseboat rocked violently and hit Mark's side of the dock with a sharp bang. Siggie's frantic barking pierced the thick fog as the momentum tossed me into the cold channel and smashed me into the side of the dock. The thick cluster of crusty barnacles attached to the wall of the dock ripped through my clothes and clawed across my skin. The water around me stained pinkish, and I prayed no sharks swam this close to shore.

Fully clothed, I sank fast as a rock. I wriggled out of

my jacket and kicked off my shoes. I shivered as something slimy slithered between my feet. I shoved my floating hair out of my face and blinked rapidly to get my bearings, but with the murky water so dark, I couldn't see my fingers in front of my eyes.

The houseboat shifted direction again and wedged me between it and the dock. I bent my legs and used my knees as leverage, but my legs weren't strong enough to move the boat. If the tide didn't work in my favor and move it, I'd be screwed. Trapped and running out of air, I'd drown in a matter of minutes. I turned my head to gauge the distance to the surface. No clue. It was impossible to accurately gauge the distance or depth in water this murky. How long I could hold my breath wasn't my only problem. In water this cold, I wouldn't last long. Five minutes ago, my biggest worry? Not having a full bottle of Chardonnay. Now? Will Muriel adopt Siggie if I die? I tamped the panic rising from my belly. Focus, I told myself. I didn't have the luxury of freaking out.

The houseboat lurched again, and I wriggled free, but as the boat moved, the keel slammed into my head. Despite the searing, incredible pain, I turned my head from side to side, trying to get my bearings, but it was a losing fight in the soupy water. I reached and lurched my way along the underbelly of the houseboat with the depth perception of a blind guy. I cleared the bow, and my heart leaped at the fighting chance of making it to the surface. I kicked out, but the belt loop on the back of my jeans got snared on the tail hook and pulled me back. Thrashing and wriggling made it worse. I unbuckled the belt, but I couldn't pull it off. I reached behind to pull the belt loop off the tailhook, but it had twisted around into a pretzel. The more I pulled it, the more tightly it snagged. I needed air. I needed it now. Seconds from passing out, black dots blurred my vision. I'd drown if the belt wouldn't come loose. Not gonna happen. I unzipped my jeans, pulled them off, and shot to the surface seconds before my lungs burst.

I hit the surface and gulped a huge lungful of the sweet air. The water level was still high, but the tide was going out. I swiveled my head searching for the dock, and a wave hit me in the face. I coughed out a mouthful of the briny channel while trying to tread water.

The air temperature dropped, and the ground fog dissipated, so I found my bearings, but a thick layer of fog still shrouded the starless sky. Only a few yards from my reach, but the dock might as well be a million miles away. Exhaustion overwhelmed me. My leaden arms proved useless for swimming a single stroke. As I faded, Siggie, my guardian angel, appeared from out of thin air. He'd jumped into the water and found me. He slipped a meaty paw under my head and kept my noggin above the water. His powerful jaws clamped onto my shirt, and he pulled me towards the dock. Bright emergency beams searching the basin blinded me. Through water-clogged ears, I made out a faint but familiar female voice who shouted, "I see them! Siggie's got her, and he's pulling her to the dock. Mark, do you see them? They're two, three yards from the houseboat, portside half-point from the stern to the bow. Siggie's five yards or so from the dock. Lie down and stretch out as far as possible to reach them." Muriel's husky voice barked the orders with the authority of a drill sergeant. "Attaboy. Grab her, but be careful. She's bleeding, so mind the way you take her onto the dock."

Two strong arms grabbed me under my armpits. I coughed and barfed another half-gallon of the channel all over myself. Two more arms wrapped around my waist and pulled me to the dock. Muriel said, "Easy now. Watch her head." They pulled me out of the water, and I shivered uncontrollably from head to toe. A blast of cold air chilled me to the bone. Muriel said, "Lay her on the towels and dry her. Once she's dry, wrap her tightly in those blankets. She's blue as a Blue Jay. Get her warm quickly, or she'll go into shock." Calloused fingers on gentle hands slid a canvas deck cushion under my head and swaddled me like a newborn in two thermal blankets. Muriel kneeled and leaned close to my head and talked. My ears hadn't drained yet, so her voice sounded as faint as a train whistle in a tunnel. I strained to hear her promise. "We've got ya now, kiddo. You're gonna be fine." Muriel's words warmed my heart, and my shaking slowed to a shiver as the heat from the blankets, and the warmth of Siggie's body stretched out his full length, glued to my side seeped deep into my bones.

Then the world went black.

****

I awoke running a scratchy tongue around a cottony mouth and fighting a splitting headache while lying in a bed that wasn't mine. Snip leaned next to me and chirped, "Good morning, sunshine. Welcome back."

Welcome back from where?

I cracked open an eye and was startled. "Holy crap," I moaned. "If I'm lying flat on my back and you're examining me, I guess I died."

Snip laughed. "You came pretty close, but you managed not to drown."

My eyes roamed around the strange room. "Where

am I?"

She said, "Marina del Rey hospital."

Last night's adventure under the channel came rushing back. I yelped, "Oh my God, Siggie and my boat! I've gotta get out of here!" I raised my head to get out of bed, and the searing pain behind my eyes had me seeing stars.

Snip eased me back onto the mattress. "Siggie is safe at your neighbor's, and your boat is fine. You're down for the count with a good-sized lump on the back of your head, a couple of cracked ribs, and lots of bumps and bruises all over your body. Lie still, if you want to recover before the next ice age."

No kidding. Every part of my body ached. Even my hair hurt. I raised my bandaged arm attached to an IV and winced. "What is this?"

Snip said, "Antibiotic to prevent infection. You're covered with some nasty cuts and bruises from those barnacles. It took the techs three-plus hours to clean all the fragments out of your cuts."

I changed positions and swore loudly.

Snip said, "Try to lie as still as possible. Your body needs to heal. You're gonna be sore for a while. You banged your head pretty hard against the hull of your boat. Take your pick of a smorgasbord of injuries causing the pain: A mild concussion, two cracked ribs, and you're a lovely shade of black and blue completely around from your boobs down to your fanny." She grinned. "If you planned to enter a marathon, forget it. You won't be running for at least a month." And they say doctors have no sense of humor.

The door opened, and AJ and Miguel walked in. AJ resembled a disaster movie survivor, and Miguel's olive complexion had turned white as a ghost.

I said, "No offense, but you two look as nasty as over-cooked crap. How long have you guys been here?" I lay back slowly. "How did I get here? The last thing I remember is falling into the drink."

AJ said, "Siggie jumped into the channel and swam you to the dock. Your neighbors pulled you out of the water and called nine-one-one."

Snip said, "We arrived here twenty minutes after the ambulance brought you in at nine last night and never left."

I asked, "And who told you guys?"

AJ said, "The harbor patrol called the LA Sheriff's office to report the incident. The deputy sheriff working on the vandalism of your houseboat called my cell phone and gave me the heads up. I called Sophie and Miguel."

I narrowed my eyes. "An *accident*, not *an incident*. My dock lines got fouled, so the boat drifted out of the slip, and she slammed into the end of the dock. I lost my balance and fell into the channel. Why get the sheriff involved in an accident?"

Miguel took the seat next to my bed and held my hand. "This was no accident. Your lines weren't fouled. Someone cut them."

AJ said, "You've pissed off somebody big time, and somebody wants you dead." AJ wagged her index finger in my face. "Won't let it happen." She grinned a lopsided grin, cratering her round face. "Peso would never forgive me."

Chapter Thirty

The way the Yentas stared at me, either I had a booger hanging out of my nose, or I'd spilled coffee on my shirt. I patted the front of my shirt. "Did I dribble coffee on myself or something?"

Joan grinned. "Yeah, or something."

Concern etched worry lines on Hope's beautiful heart-shaped face. "You doin' okay?"

"Yeah. Okay." I wrinkled my forehead. "Honestly, I have no idea why they kept me in the hospital for two nights."

Sonia gave me the stink eye. "All those black and blue marks and bandages. Not your best look."

Joan said, "No offense, but when were you flattened by a bus?"

I grimaced. "Cut out the wisecracks. It hurts to laugh."

Hope said, "With a head injury, it's better to be on the side of caution, especially if you live alone."

I said, "The doctor refused to release me with no one to watch me the first two nights. So, Siggie stayed at Muriel's, and I went to Queenie's."

I touched the back of my head. "The big lump shrank down to hardly noticeable. The scalp around it is a bit tender, especially while brushing my hair. It is still hard to take a deep breath with the cracked ribs. Add some bumps and bruises from the barnacles and getting pulled onto the dock to the list, but all things considered, it could have been a lot worse."

Joan said, "Yeah. No kidding. How about being dead?"

Queenie said, "I'd say you're a cat with nine lives, but you're allergic to kitties."

I said, "Lady luck had me covered. If the zipper on my jeans had stuck, I'd have drowned." I smiled. "Good thing I walk as much as I do."

Sonia said, "Speaking of lucky, any luck nailing whoever messed with your boat?"

My shoulders slumped. "Not exactly. A few clues, but no smoking gun."

Joan wiggled her digits. "What about fingerprints?"

I groused. "Oh yeah. Lots of them. Unfortunately, most of them are mine. Several partials on the aft deck and a thumbprint on the cleat hitch, but so far, no match to the prints to anyone in the system. With no other physical evidence to tie anyone to the crime, the police can't demand a fingerprint sample. They can ask, but you're not obligated to provide it. It has to be volunteered."

Sonia narrowed her eyes. "If Lynnie or Carrie refused to give their fingerprints, it makes them look guilty."

I nodded. "In the court of public opinion, they'd be tried and convicted. Unfortunately, it's not a crime to decline a request, so without a warrant to compel them, in a court of law, they'd be in the clear."

A frown wrinkled Joan's face. "A few unidentified fingerprints, is it?"

I fingered my shirt sleeve. "They found a small piece of torn fabric attached to the underside of the horn of the cleat hitch. It's not from my wardrobe, so it has to belong to whoever messed the lines. The cops asked if I recognized it, but with a scrap so small, it's impossible to tell if I'd seen it on someone before. Who knows if they'll ever trace it to anyone?"

Sonia asked, "Are you back on the boat?"

I played a teaspoon rata-tat-tat drumroll on the table. "The sheriff's office released her an hour ago. I'll sleep in my bed tonight."

Hope shuddered. "Is it wise to go back on the houseboat? First the dead rats and now this. How will you ever feel safe on it again?"

I gave her an odd look. "The houseboat is my home. While I appreciated Queenie taking me in, I wouldn't want to overstay my welcome." I glanced at Queenie and laughed. "I'm sure those pampered two cats of hers are tired of camping in the garage."

Concern creased Joan's forehead. "What is there to prevent someone from doing it again?"

I said, "I replaced the damaged lines with a security spring action, and now the forward lines come with a steel center core running through them. Unless somebody has heavy-duty cable cutters, those lines are not getting cut. The outer shell of the rope might be breached, but not the lines. Before I board, I will check the lines to make sure they are securely tied onto the cleat hitch. Both the forward and aft doors are already secured with double locks, and wooden poles between the sliding glass doors prevent a break-in. The dockmaster changed the lock on the security gate, and marina security agreed to make an extra round at our basin. That's about it."

Hope said, "You considered selling the houseboat and buying a real home?"

I gave her the stink eye. "My houseboat *is* a real home. It's *my* home. I love living on the water. It's peaceful and beautiful. It's the life I've chosen, and no one is going to scare me out of it. If I sold the boat and ran, whoever is responsible for this wins. I'd never let it happen. So, no. I'm not going anyplace else. I'm already at the place where I want to be."

Chapter Thirty-One

I finished everything critically important. As to the rest? Tomorrow is another day. For once, I'd get out of the office at a decent time. Messenger bag packed, car keys out, the cell phone in my blazer pocket, and visions of a pepperoni pizza and Chardonnay propelling me out the door.

One foot into the hall, and the phone rang. Crap. One ring, two, a third. I checked out the hallway. A string of dark offices. The rest of the aisle had already vacated the premises for the night. No witnesses. No one to say, "Hey, your phone's ringing," and guilt me into answering. Screw 'em. Whoever it was, let them call back tomorrow. And yet, the big wuss that I am, my feet stayed cemented to the spot in the doorjamb. If I didn't answer, I'd be awake all night obsessing about the damned call. Three rings. Four rings. This was one relentless caller or somebody mighty impressed by their self-importance. Toss a coin.

I sighed and dropped into my chair and checked the Caller ID. AJ is at the other end of the line. No doubt reporting, yet again, all the progress that is not being made. Why does she bother calling? More importantly, why do I bother answering? I hit the speakerphone function and sighed into the phone. "I hope this is important. There's a pizza with my name on it getting cold even as we speak."

AJ huffed. "If the pizza is so important, by all means, go on. Far be it from me to get between you and your pie."

I tamped back the excitement. This wasn't my first rodeo. Things important to AJ often meant nothing to me. But for giggles and squeaks, I bit. "The pizza will keep. What's so important?"

Excitement raised the timbre of her voice. "The wheels of justice sometimes turn slowly, but they do turn. The sheriff got the report back on those prints from your boat. It took a little longer to get a match, but we got one. You were right. Lynnie Stubbs wasn't who vandalized your boat. The thumbprint on your cleat belongs to Carrie Le Beau."

Whoa. I moved the phone base to the edge of my desk and spun my seat around. I put my feet on a step stool and settled in. Good thing my curiosity got the best of me, and I answered the phone. "Really? You said they ran Carrie's name through the system, and nothing registered. How could they get the match?"

AJ said, "When her name failed to show up in our county system, they ran a state-wide search. It took so long because the incident goes back a few years. Hold on a sec. Lemme get the report." AJ rustled the papers. "Incident happened in San Diego. Nothing major. The report says she got arrested at an animal-rights protest. Charges were eventually dropped, but lucky for us, her prints weren't deleted from the system."

I burst out laughing. "So, she's in the system for getting busted at an animal-rights protest, and *that* nailed her for putting dead rats on my boat? Ya gotta love the irony. So, this means she's the one who put the rats on the boat and cut my lines?"

AJ said, "Yes, ma'am."

At least my instincts were right about Lynnie. "And the next step?"

AJ said, "Next step is we get a warrant, search her house, and let the system work. Depending on the evidence we find, the charges range from vandalism to attempted murder."

I said, "So she's not a suspect in Jack's murder?"

AJ said, "Yes, and no."

I looked at the phone wonky. "Huh?"

"So far, Mr. Workman is the guy. Once the paperwork is complete, the DA is set to go before the grand jury at the end of the week and expects no problem getting an indictment. Ms. Le Beau's prints match the ones on the juice containers in the refrigerator at the victim's house. We're still waiting for the report on the ones on the vial at Mr. Tyne's home. As of now, those remain unidentified. We found some latent prints on the two containers confiscated from Mr. Workman's office, but they aren't a match to Ms. Le Beau."

I bunched my shoulders. "If the latent prints on David's containers and the vial at Jack's house aren't David's or Carrie's, they must be someone's."

AJ said, "Other than Mr. Tyne's, the prints on the vial at the victim's house are a mystery. They don't belong to anyone who lives in the house. We won't know until the rest of the report comes in. As to Mr. Workman's vial, the prints might belong to Mr. Workman's wife or the guy who details his car."

I racked my brain for a compelling reason to murder Jack Tyne. The answer? Loss and revenge. My synapses snapped with the zip of live wires in an electric storm as the pieces of the puzzle all fell into place. My heart twisted into square knots. Oh. My. God. No. I might not have it all, but I had enough. Dang it. "AJ," I sighed, "Trust me. David isn't the killer. I figured out who murdered Jack, and it breaks my heart."

The line went dead as a hand reached from behind my shoulder and disconnected the phone. Then the cold barrel of a gun dug into the back of my head.

Regret tinged Lynnie's ice-cold voice. "You should have let the phone ring and gone for the pizza."

I choked on the words. "Lynnie, tell me why?"

She spat, "I got tired of everything that was mine being taken away from me."

Lynnie, who Jack fired. Lynnie, who David betrayed.

Lynnie, whose nose got rubbed in it by Carrie, the woman who stole her job.

Lynnie, with nothing left to lose. So, Lynnie plotted her revenge.

Lynnie brought a care package to Carrie's cottage. While at Carrie's house, Lynnie helped herself to Grandpa Le Beau's blood thinners and the rat poison in Carrie's garage. Lynnie went to Jack's house to pay her condolences to Mo Mac and switched out Jack's pain medication for the blood-thinner pills. Those were her prints on the vial.

No one else is in the office but Lynnie at the crack of dawn. Arrogant David doesn't lock his office. After all, who is dumb enough to invade his privacy? Lynnie plants the rat poison and blood thinner pills in David's office and waits. Jack first has coffee with David and the second round in his office at the same time every day.

Lynnie spikes rat poison into Jack's coffee.

Lynnie plants the vial of blood thinners inside her

desk to frame Carrie.

Lynnie punishes Carrie, David, and Jack for their sins. Revenge is sweet.

The jangle of the phone ringing cut through the tension with the sharpness of a blade.

By reflex, I half turned to reach for the receiver. Lynnie jabbed the gun barrel into the base of my skull. "Don't even try."

I glanced at the caller ID. AJ calling back. "Lynnie, it's AJ. She figures we were cut off. If I don't answer it, she'll realize something is wrong."

Lynnie snorted. "So, who cares? By the time she arrives, it won't matter."

I swallowed back the bile rising to my throat but gagged on the words. "Why not?"

I shook off an involuntary shudder as she pushed the gun barrel into my skull even harder. "It'll be too late to help you."

The phone stopped ringing, and my heart sank.

Keep her talking. "I haven't told her anything. Put the gun down and walk out before you do something you can't undo."

"Too late. What's done is done." She snarled. "You kept sticking your nose every place it didn't belong. There's no choice now."

I used her own words against her. "You once told me everyone has choices. You were right. It's not too late for you to make the right one. Make the smart choice and walk out now."

The phone rang again.

I pleaded. "Lynnie, *please*…"

Her angry voice snapped with the same cruelty as the crack of a whip. "Forget it. Get up."

If I got up, my goose is cooked. "Ok. Let me tie my shoelace first."

She sighed impatiently. "Fine, but make it snappy."

As I bent to tie my shoe, I put my left hand in my blazer pocket and grabbed my cell phone. I closed my eyes in concentration. Hopefully, I hadn't called the recording for the correct time. I maxed the volume and prayed Snip worked late.

Lynnie smacked the barrel of the gun sharply across my scalp. "Come on already. It doesn't take this long to tie one shoelace. I said get up!"

"All right already, don't get nervous," said the one with the gun barrel digging into the back of her head.

She tapped the gun more gently on my head. "Turn around slowly and give me your phone."

I trusted her. I believed in her. I stood up for her. I protected her. I defended her. Her betrayal broke my heart and crushed my soul. I said in a voice so calm I didn't recognize it as mine, "It's in a recessed zipped compartment on the inside of my messenger bag, so it's hard to find. Let me get it out."

She snapped her fingers and barked. "Not a chance. Let me have it."

Maybe the menace of her tone did it? Or maybe it was the arrogance of the words themselves? All the empathy and feeling once in my heart for Lynnie Stubbs died in a heartbeat. The will to live took over. Only one of us is going to come out of this vertical. It will not be Lynnie Stubbs.

I pushed my laptop to the front of the messenger bag and tightened my grip on the strap. I readily agreed. "Sure, no problem. I'll let you have it."

Before she realized I had no intention of handing it

to her, I stood and whirled around. With my outrage powering the force, I smashed the messenger bag into Lynnie's face with all my might. The loud crunch of her nose breaking reminded me of the snap of a crisp celery stick. The geyser of blood gushed out and squirted a red spray reminiscent of the fountain in the center of the Echo Park Lake gone wild. Lynnie screamed her head off and dropped the gun. The blast of the shot boomed with the volume of a bomb when the gun fell to the floor. A bullet whizzed past my head and shattered the computer screen. My ears rang loud as a fire alarm as I hurdled over Lynnie's prone body and ran for my life.

Chapter Thirty-Two

I raced the length of the executive office hall as if my pants had caught fire. Lynnie might be down, but she wouldn't be for long. I reached the end of the hall and had a decision to make. Go to the right and the main corridor to the lobby, or the left and the warehouse?

Logic said there was no decision. Get to the front door and keep going...if I had my purse and messenger bag. Along with them, my keys were in my office. So much for an escape by car. The alternative? Hoof it from our factory located on a side street until I hit the main drag. Our factory is in an industrial area between the apparel mart and the produce market. I checked the time, and my heart pulsed in my throat. The mart is a ghost town by now, and the produce district bustled from two in the morning until two in the afternoon. This time of night, the area is deserted. No place was open, and no one was around to help. Worst case scenario? A druggie lurking in the shadows waiting for someone to mug. I shook the scary scenario off.

No keys, but I still had my phone. I chanced a peek at the battery level. I sighed with relief. Three bars. I called AJ on her cell phone and the office, but she didn't pick up at either place. I left a message and hoped she checked her voicemail more often than me. I called Snip as well, but either she was with a patient or gone for the day. She didn't pick up when I called her voicemail either, so I left a message at both places and hoped for the best. I texted them both and prayed one of them saw my message. But for now at least, I was on my own.

The warehouse was twice the size of the factory and occupied a city block. I've spent many hours at the warehouse supervising incoming goods and outgoing orders. Unlike Lynnie, I was familiar with every inch of the huge, cavernous building. Fifty rows of products packed tightly together on hanging racks stacked to the ceiling on four floors provided plenty of places to get lost and never get found. I'd get to the top level and head for the back corner. Camouflaged between the beach accessories and bikinis, I'd call in the cavalry, and wait for the all-clear.

Lynnie's screams echoing through the halls sent a shudder that traveled from the top of my head to the tips of my toes. I turned onto the aisle for the warehouse and ran fast as a sprinter with Lynnie Stubbs not far behind.

****

Jack had insisted his team needed a design studio separate from the other divisions, but no open space was available in the main section of the factory. So, the production department carved out an oddly conical-shaped design studio with a narrow entrance and a wide work space between the fabric storage area and the warehouse entrance.

Once Jack's team got let go, we debated whether or not to move the juniors and kids design studio back to the design department in the factory. In the interest of time and the effort needed to disassemble the one and move everything to the factory, we kept the juniors and kids design studio in place until the end of the season.

The warehouse crew opened the building at six in

the morning and left at three in the afternoon. Now, three hours later, no one was still in the warehouse. If I speed walked, it took me a good ten minutes from my office to the GOOFYFOOT design studio. If I couldn't cut the time in half, Lynnie would catch up with me. I had the element of surprise in my favor. She didn't know my location or have any idea where I was headed. But with a highly motivated Lynnie Stubbs running after me on legs a lot longer than mine, time wasn't on my side. The hall from the fabric storage area to the design studio had no illumination, save the floor lights installed, so no one walked into the walls. To get to the warehouse entrance from the inside of the factory, you had to pass the GOOFYFOOT design studio.

The studio lights beamed brightly ahead at the end of the long hall. I strained to hear a female voice coming from the studio. The voice sounded familiar, but whose? The voice took a desperate tone and got louder. I stopped for another listen. Carrie Le Beau screaming her head off for somebody to help her. Huh? My first impulse? Keep going. I had enough problems of my own. Save my tush and not worry about Carrie. Why risk my neck for someone who nearly succeeded in getting me killed? Let her learn first-hand that God helps those who help themselves. I ran a few feet past the design studio, and Nana's face floated in front of me. I sighed and stepped through the studio door. I nearly tripped over Carrie, bound to the chair behind the design table from her ankles to her armpits by a series of ropes made out of strips of swimwear fabric. A sample-stuffed rolling rack sat on her left. Three GOOFYFOOT surfboards leaned against the wall next to her on the right. Her bleeding lower lip swelled to the size of a half-inflated balloon. A thin ribbon of blood dripped to her cheek from a nasty gash on her forehead. Her left eye swelled half shut, with the start of an ugly, purplish-tinged shiner. She lifted her lolling head to see if Lynnie returned. Fear lines cratered her face until her one good eye focused enough to see me.

I asked, "Why on earth are you here?"

She snarked. "Obviously, not for the square dancing."

Everyone's a comedian. "I don't have time for any of your crap. Give me a straight answer, or untie yourself."

She said, "Ok, ok. Let's not have a cow. Lynnie called a few hours ago with a lead on a job. She told me to bring my portfolio and meet her in the GOOFYFOOT design studio. She didn't say the name of the company with the job or why she needed to see my portfolio, and I didn't ask. I didn't care. I haven't even had a bad offer to refuse. I'm almost out of money and desperate for work. So, I asked no questions. I grabbed the portfolio and broke every traffic law to get here before she changed her mind. I put the portfolio on the table, and the next thing I knew, Lynnie whacked me on the back of the head with a gun. I came to strapped to this chair."

I knelt in front of her. "We've gotta high step it big time. I slowed Lynnie down some, but she isn't far behind. Can you run?"

Carrie sneered, "Why not?" Carrie touched the nasty lump on her noggin and winced. "She pistol-whipped my head, not my feet." She lifted her feet and danced a little kick to demonstrate.

I muttered, "Cochon," under my breath. I should have ignored Nana and kept going. Too late now. I untied her and tested out the theory of strength in numbers to work in my favor…unless I beat Lynnie to the punch and strangled Carrie myself.

Chapter Thirty-Three

The deafening crack of the gunshot echoed around the oddly-shaped design room. Carrie screamed as the bullet whizzed over her head and pierced the wall behind her left shoulder. My heartbeat thundered in my ears as I dove under the design table. A minute passed, and no more gunshots rang, so I pulled myself out. The good news? Carrie and I were still breathing. The bad news? The odds for our survival? Slimsky to nonesky.

Lynnie laughed. "I wanted to make sure I had your full attention now." Carrie nodded with the speed of a spastic bobblehead doll. Lynnie pointed the gun at me. Her broken nose garbled her speech, and some of the words came out as if Elmer Fudd was talking while underwater. "I appweciate you pwaying superhero. Having us all together is so much easier than pwaying hide and go seek."

I took a deep bow and muttered, "I live to serve." And she cackled with the laugh of an evil crone.

With her one eye ringed by a greenish and purple shiner and swollen shut, Lynnie resembled a Frankenstein wannabe. The other eye dilated wonky wild, like a junkie high on drugs. Her broken nose lay flopped to the side of her face, reminiscent of an undercooked sausage. Her blood-splotched face contorted as Lynnie's maniacal laugh came out the same as a hyena on crack.

She waved the barrel of the gun around as if conducting an orchestra. I followed the arc of the gun past Carrie's head. Lynnie's shot had blown a big chunk of plaster from the wall above the rolling rack. Carrie shook her head, and pieces of plaster flew out of her hair, scattering helter-skelter across the design studio floor.

Lynnie aimed the gun at Carrie's chest. "Next one is gonna be a bullseye in the middle of your heart. Oops, my bad." Lynnie giggled as maniacally as the madwoman she turned out to be. Lynnie raised the gun barrel level to Carrie's forehead. "Can't shoot you in the heart. You don't have one."

Carrie's voice caught. "Why me? I've never done anything to you."

Lynnie sputtered. "O-Oh, c-come on, don't be an i-idiot." Lynnie gave Carrie the big eye. "Wight fwom the beginning you've twied evewything possible to tank my caweer. At the Fashion Institute, you stole my design idea for the senior pwoject." Lynnie snarled, "And your award? All mine."

"Listen up, scholarship girlie." Carrie sneered, "You're jealous of my talent. Every design I submitted? All original, all mine." Carrie pointed to the rack full of samples and snarked, "You couldn't design yourself out of a paper bag. Some bleeding-heart administrator took pity on you and made you her feel-good project. It's the only way you'd get into the school."

Geesh, for crying out loud, Carrie, smooth move. Why don't you piss her off a little more? How could you miss the gun she's pointing at your head?

"You shut your mouf! It's a filthy lie." Lynnie growled. "You got into the school wying on your back. I *earned* my pwace in the pwogram. Not exactly a state secret you scwewed the dean of design." Lynnie barked a bitter laugh. "You won the award for Most Pwomising Designer all wight. You pwomised to scwew the dean silly in exchange for high gwades."

Carrie pushed her boobs out and wiggled her ass.

Too bad I untied her.

Carrie pointed to her chest. "Betcha wish these were your best assets." Carrie squeezed her girls together and laughed. "If these babies worked it for ya, no need to study so hard."

Lynnie, do us both a favor and tape Carrie's mouth shut.

Lynnie waved the gun at the rolling rack. "First you steal my school pwoject, and next you steal my job."

I inched closer to the surfboards while those two wackos went at one another in their verbal game of ping pong.

Carrie tsked her disdain. "You're such a moron. How could I steal your job? I had no idea you worked at Mermaid." Carrie's face turned an alarming shade of red. "You and that worthless piece of crap Jack ruined *my* career, you talentless bitch." Carrie pointed her index finger at her chest. "I'm the victim. If anything, you stole the job from me."

Lynnie grinned. "The job hunt going gweat so far, Cawie? Any wuck?"

Carrie's shoulders slumped. "As if you need to ask."

Lynnie spat. "Some nove asking me to help you find a job." Lynnie rolled her eyes. "As if." Lynnie smiled pure evil as she pointed to her back. "One of your interviewers cawed for a weference, and I gwadly told them exactwy how you got your last job." Lynnie snorted, and a stream of blood squirted out of her nostrils. "Guess using me as a weference was not your best move."

Carrie pointed at the gun aimed at her head. "You wanted to kill someone, ya shoulda killed Jack. He's the one who fired you, not me." Staring death in the face started getting to Carrie? She pointed to herself and laughed. "Oh, wait. It's too late. I already took care of it for you."

My jaw barely missed hitting the ground as Lynnie screamed, "You didn't kill him!" Lynnie tapped the barrel of the gun to her chest. "Me, me, me! I killed him, not you. I did it. Me, me! Not you! Me!"

Come on, Lynnie. Get a little more excited, and shoot yourself. Hope springs eternal.

Lynnie waved the gun from side to side as if it were a lantern. "You've alweady taken evewything else fwom me. And now you're gonna take the cwedit for killing the SOB? Not gonna happen."

Carrie's facial expression bore the same level of disgust given to a cockroach found in a picnic basket. Carrie taunted. "You expect me to believe a sniveling wimp like you suddenly turned into a stone-cold killer? Not in a million years." Carrie snarked, "How did you do it? Kill him with kindness? Bring him some of your grandma's goodies, hoping he'd eat himself to death?"

I dunno, from my perch in the cheap seats, Lynnie's gun looked pretty intimidating. Not a brain surgeon's choice of words to make. Carrie either had a death wish or ice water flowing in her veins. Or maybe she just had nothing left to lose.

Lynnie spat her disgust. "Dat idiot Jack. So pwedictable. Evewy morning, he went to the men's woom at 8:30. While he took his daily constitutional, I snuck into his office and spiked his coffee. I used the wat poison I stole from your gawage." Lynnie cocked a brow. "Missing your gwandpa's meds? I helped myself to them too. I twied my best to set you and Jack's missus up for Jack's murder." Lynnie glared at me. "Unfortunately, Nancy Dwew kept scwewing up all of my pwans, so I fwamed David."

I took a mental bow.

Newfound respect shone in Carrie's eyes. "No kidding? While you poisoned Jack's coffee, I sprinkled it into his juice." Carrie narrowed her eyes. "You put the blood thinners into the vial in Jack's bathroom?"

Lynnie jutted her jaw proudly. "Damned wight. I paid a condolence call, and after a bit, I asked to use the bathwoom. I swapped out the pills in the vial for the ones I stole fwom your cottage."

Carrie tapped the side of her head. "You took it? I went to frame you, but the vial vanished. I tore the cottage apart looking for it. I used Gramp's last vial planting it in your desk drawer. "Carrie narrowed her eyes. "You tried to frame Jack's wife?" She gave Lynnie an appreciative round of applause. "Hilarious. Me too." She burst out laughing. "Great minds think alike."

Great minds, all right. If you're Bonnie and Clyde. This wacko episode had turned into a regular lovefest. Next, they'll be making lunch plans. Cripes.

Lynnie said, "Jack's a coffee addict. He always had a cup in his hand." Lynnie sniffed. "He didn't dwink much juice in a day." Lynnie puffed out her chest like she expected a medal. "My spiking his coffee evewy day killed him."

Carrie laughed evilly. "You helped him along, but the night before he died, I screwed his brains out and put enough poison in his drink to kill an army." Carrie proudly tapped her heart. "Believe me, I'm the one who made sure he'd be dead the next morning."

My head swung back and forth watching these two maniacs one-upping each other, but time ran out. We'd arrived at a game, a set, and a match. Lynnie had no problem admitting her guilt. Why? The answer was terrifyingly elementary. She had no intention of letting Carrie or me live long enough to tell the cops.

Why is a cop never around when you need one? They say ask, and ye shall receive. The answer pinged loudly from inside my jacket pocket. Lynnie waggled her fingers and glared. "Give it." She aimed the gun at my head. "Take it out nice and swow. No funny stuff this time, or I'll bwow your head off."

I gauged my chances. A bullet trumps a sleight of hand every time. I took the phone out of my pocket and glanced at the face. The text? From AJ. —*Hold on. Help is coming.*— I hit delete and handed Lynnie the phone.

Lynnie's one good eye winked open and shut the same as a blinking traffic signal. Missing the irony, she said, "I'm not bwind. You deweted the message. Doesn't matter. You two are toast, and I'll be wong gone by the time your wescuers awwive." She grinned. "But better safe than sowwy." She dropped my cell on the ground and crushed it under the heel of her shoe. For good measure, she ripped the cord out of the landline on the desk and put it in her jeans back pocket.

Carrie turned to me and giggled at her joke. "Love the way I decorated your boat?"

Lynnie's jaw went slack, and I turned stone-faced.

Carrie shook her blonde hair and smiled smugly at Lynnie. "I wore a dark, curly wig and put a beauty mark on my lip. The resemblance? Simply amazing."

Her explanation certainly explained a lot.

She patted her girls and smiled like a shark. "Of course, I taped down the ladies, so they'd lie flat as your little titties."

This dopey nutcase must have a death wish. What do they say? Sometimes, God punishes us by granting us our wishes? She had an excellent chance of hers being granted, and soon.

Carrie stomped her foot. "Get it? Rats for a Rat?" Carrie rolled her eyes. "You guys are so dense. I guess I better spell it out for you." She pointed to me and poked quote marks in the air. "Ratted. Jack. And. Carrie. Out."

Lynnie shrank back in horror. "My God, Cawwie. Who does something so awful?"

So, Lynnie, no problem shooting me dead, but you're outraged by Carrie putting rats on my boat? Nonetheless, it begged the question. Yeah, Carrie. Let's hear your answer.

Carrie bared her teeth like a cornered dog. "Easy. Payback for getting Jack and me fired."

If I asked sweetly? "Lynnie, please let me borrow the gun."

Lynnie shook her head. "You and Jack got yourselves fired all on your own. You didn't need anyone's help."

Finally, something we agreed on.

Lynnie aimed the business end of the gun at Carrie's head. "And now you're gonna pay for everything you've done."

Carrie steepled her fingers and whimpered a prayer.

No kidding, Carrie. Now is a dandy time to start.

Lynnie focused on Carrie too much to pay much

attention to me, but not for long. The time had come to make my move. I prayed Lynnie wouldn't notice, or Carrie react, as I crept toward the surfboards.

Keep her talking, I silently coached Carrie.

"Lynnie, I'm sorry." Carrie choked out a sob. "Please don't do this."

Now you try contrition? Geesh, Carrie. Pathetic whining is the best you came up with? Lynnie ought to shoot you and take us both out of our misery.

I slowly inched baby steps to the surfboards stacked next to the design table. The choices reminded me of Goldilocks and the Three Bears. The longboard stood a foot taller than me. Never happen. The boogie board? Too light to inflict enough damage. The shortboard fit the bill perfectly.

Lynnie held the gun barrel steady and aimed at Carrie's head. She looked through the sight using her one good eye and cocked the gun's hammer. I caught a break. Her other eye swelled shut. Once again, I had the element of surprise in my favor. The time? Now or never. I aimed. Her head? The preferred prime target, but out of the question. She'd get off a shot before I could raise the board high enough. So, I aimed for her gut. Before her peripheral vision caught my movement, I rammed the fin of the shortboard into Lynnie's breadbasket with the power of a wrecking ball. The air whooshed out of Lynnie's lungs, and she deflated like a pinpricked balloon. She folded as fast as a cheap card table and dropped the gun. The gunshot boomed and shook the room with the force of a thunderclap. Carrie's earsplitting scream ricocheted off the design room walls, reminiscent of a horror movie echo chamber, as she collapsed in a bloody heap.

Chapter Thirty-Four

I dropped the surfboard and kicked the gun across the room like Pele scoring the winning goal at the World Cup. The gun landed on the fin side of the longboard and in front of the design room door. Lynnie groaned and coughed up some blood, trying to roll onto her side. She kicked out, and the heel of her shoe caught my knee as I jumped on her back. I tried to get her in a chokehold, but my angle was a tad off-kilter. Lynnie bucked wild as an unbroken bronco. I'd barely recovered from my houseboat injuries, so stamina was one thing in short supply. My aching arms went as limp as cooked spaghetti. Every time my knee moved, sharp arrows of pain shot from my femur to the top of my spine. Holding her down much longer was not gonna happen.

I eyed the gun lying near the door. Mental head slap. I am such a moron. Why kick it and not grab it? If she lifted her head and looked to the right, Lynnie would see the gun too. My biceps seized, and any minute she'd buck me off. My knee had swelled to the size of a tennis ball. I'd be in no shape to catch her, even if she crawled and reached the gun. I could not let that happen.

I desperately searched for something to tie her up with. I put my good knee into the small of Lynnie's back and leaned over her left side towards the design table. I extended my left arm out, but I was a long way from the edge of the table. Lynnie grabbed my right wrist and twisted. I punched her hard in the jaw with my left, and her body went slack. Her jaw might be made of glass, but my left hand throbbed as if I'd punched a brick wall. I shook out my fist to ease the stinging and flexed my fingers to make sure my knuckles weren't broken. Three of her teeth lay next to her bloodied mouth. Cripes.

I leaned past Lynnie's torso and stretched, but I lacked at least half a yard. Unless I grew the wingspan of a condor, I'd never reach it. Time and options diminished more with every tick of the clock. Lynnie wouldn't be out much longer.

Carrie lay dead still next to the design table. She hadn't so much as twitched. "Carrie," I yelled. "Are you all right?" No reply. I yelled louder. "Carrie, can you hear me?" Still no response. Not that it mattered. Either case, dead or alive, I'd get no help from Carrie. I looked back at Lynnie and shivered. I had a much bigger fish to land, and I'd better land it soon.

I took a chance Lynnie wouldn't come to right then. I grabbed her by the belt and dragged her dead weight until I reached the design table. I snatched two rolls of elastic and a pair of fabric shears off the corner and pulled Lynnie's limp arms behind her back. I bent her rubbery legs back at the knees and pulled them to her pliable arms. I used my right knee to hold her extremities in place while I hacked off a goodly length of elastic. I hogtied her wrists and ankles together in tight sailor reef knots. She could writhe and wiggle around forever, but she'd never get out. I wound the second roll of elastic around her body and bound Lynnie in a butterfly loop. When I finished trussing her, Lynnie resembled a cross between a lassoed rodeo calf and an Egyptian mummy.

Chapter Thirty-Five

I squirmed in my seat, trying to find a comfortable position. My arms still ached from holding onto Lynnie for dear life. My knuckles swelled as big as ripe kumquats, and the ace bandage wrapped around my knee was wound too tight. I'm a southpaw, but with my left hand out of commission, I ate with my right. I missed my mouth half the time. I took a sip of java, and Hope dabbed a napkin at the spot I'd dribbled coffee onto my chin. Geesh. Next, she'll be feeding me lunch.

Queenie took a healthy glug of coffee and tried not to laugh as she observed me behind the rim of her mug. "Lemme get this straight. You shoved a surfboard into her belly. You jumped on her back to hold her, you punched her lights out, and you used a roll of elastic to tie her up with?"

I nodded. "Yep, I hogtied her tight as a rodeo calf." I wiggled my eyebrows. "Pretty tricky, huh? Call me the MacGyver of Mermaid. It took two hospital orderlies a half hour to cut through all the elastic." I grinned. "Living on a houseboat has its benefits. I tie a mean sailor's knot."

I was rewarded with a famous Queenie cackle for a job well done. "Unreal." Queenie raised her cup in a toast. "To you, Mac Schlivnik." She clucked her tongue. "And I managed to miss all the fun."

I laughed out loud. "If you call such madness fun,

you're as nuts as the two of them. They both *seemed* normal, but they turned out to be two bent-in-the-head, vindictive, crazy-as-a-bedbug, wackadoodle loons."

Sonia's eyes searched the breadth of the bustling coffee shop, as though she expected to see Carrie and Lynnie seated at one of the tables. Her gaze returned to our table, and she dipped her head towards me. "So, what happened to them?"

I said, "The EMT guy splinted Lynnie's nose, but she wasn't admitted into the hospital. She is currently safely behind bars."

Hope made a whirling motion around her head. "And the other crazy one?"

I pursed my lips. "Carrie is another story. The bullet nicked a few vital organs, and she lost a lot of blood. She'll be out of the hospital prison ward at the end of the week. Just in time for her indictment. AJ is confident they're both gonna go to prison for a long time."

Joan shook her head. "You and these crazies. You're a magnet for maniacs."

The truth hurts. Remarkably, Lynnie isn't the first crazed killer I'd fought off. While working at Ditzy Swimwear, I shoved a heavy rolling rack full of swimsuits into an insane buyer wielding a gun.

Hope's jaw hung open wide as a castle drawbridge. "So, they *both* admitted killing Jack?"

I snorted my coffee. "Admitted it? They *argued* as to *which one* of them killed him." I shuddered. "Wild, but funny in a terrifying kind of way." I laughed. "You'd swear they worked together. Carrie made some juice concoction Jack loved and laced it with thallium, a very potent blood thinner exterminators used to kill rats. Lynnie used the same poison to lace Jack's coffee every morning."

Joan dipped her head. "Not exactly everyday items one keeps around the house."

I grinned. "No kidding. Snip said thallium is so dangerous that it has been banned from use in this country. Carrie's grandfather kept the thallium in the cottage garage in an old plastic container and used it years ago as rat poison. Lynnie delivered a care package of food from her grandmother to Carrie and pinched the rat poison from Carrie's garage. Carrie mixed the poison in a few containers of the nectar and juice concoction for Jack. He took it home and poured it into a thermos he took to the beach and drank it each morning. Thallium is colorless and tasteless, so the guy never realized he drank poison. Jack was a big man. He tolerated small doses of the poison with no visible reactions. Lynnie spiked his coffee every morning, so he got double the dosage of poison. The poor jerk lost his hair, and his gums bled, and he couldn't figure out why."

Queenie scrunched her nose. "I'd go to the doctor. Why didn't he?"

I lifted a shoulder. "Dunno. He's a typical vain guy? Or maybe too embarrassed to ask a doctor why he lost his hair? Instead, he jammed the logo cap on his head, and presto, problem solved. The blood thinner is Carrie's grandfather's AFIB prescription to prevent him from having a stroke. Carrie kept a supply of it for him at the cottage for an emergency in case he ran out. Carrie used the blood thinner as a ringer to try to frame Jack's wife. When Mo Mac got released from jail, Carrie planted it in Lynnie's desk to frame her." I widened my eyes. "It turns out Carrie and Lynnie both tried to frame Mo Mac. The lab identified both of their fingerprints on the vial in

Jack's bathroom."

Sonia narrowed her eyes. "So, Carrie must have broken in to get the pills into Jack's house?"

I shook my head no. "Nope. Carrie talked her way in by using a BS story she wanted to apologize for her screwing around with Jack. Carrie laid it on pretty thick about not being a home-wrecker and burst into well-practiced crocodile tears. Carrie excused herself to the powder room and planted the blood thinner in Jack's prescription medicine vial. Lynnie made a condolence call and used the powder room. She put more of the blood thinner in the same vial and added her fingerprints to it." I shuddered. "Carrie blamed me for getting her and Jack fired. To retaliate, she put all those rats on my boat."

Joan leaned forward in her seat. "Wait a minute. Carrie vandalized your boat? Isn't Lynnie the one your neighbor described?"

I nodded. "Yes, Muriel described Lynnie to a T. During a search of Carrie's beach cottage, AJ found a dark wig and makeup hidden in the back of a closet. Carrie disguised herself to look like Lynnie in the hopes the real Lynnie would get blamed. Carrie wouldn't know Lynnie and I share the same birthday, and the wrong birth date was a big blinking red light. But sloppiness and inattention to detail were ultimately her undoing. Her fingerprints were on the cleat hitch and the boat deck."

Confusion clouded Sonia's eyes. "But you said Lynnie had been on your boat. So, weren't her prints on it too?"

I said, "Yes, but in the interior of the cabin, specifically on the galley table and inside the head. The police found Carrie's on the exterior at the points of the damage. The smarter of the two, careful and calculating

Lynnie left nothing to tie her to the murder at her house or in her car. She hid the poison in plain sight in our factory test lab and used a test lab vial no one questioned to pour the poison into Jack's coffee every day. Jack made it easy for her by going to the men's room every day at the same time. She snuck into his office and added the rat poison to his second cup of daily java."

Joan raised her hand and waved it around, schoolgirl style. "You found rat poison in the closet in Lynnie's office, right?"

I said, "Yes. She explained it by saying there had been a recurrence of a rat infestation in the test lab."

Hope asked, "Was there a rat infestation reoccurrence?"

"Nope."

Sonia said, "Say Lynnie planted the rats herself…"

I shook my head no. "Anyone else, I'd agree. But Lynnie had a real aversion to rats going back to her childhood time she spent at her grandparent's house near the beach." I said, "Lynnie focused on revenge, and it drove every decision she made. For allowing Jack to fire her, Lynnie blamed David as much as Jack for losing her design job. She murdered Jack and framed David and paid them both back for doing her harm. She got to work every day at six A.M. The same time as the guys in the warehouse. No one else in the executive wing gets in as early as her. It's no secret David's office is never locked. He made a big deal of his open-door policy. With no one around to see her do it, Lynnie went into David's office to frame him. She found the auto soap container and the medicine vial and planted the blood thinners and rat poison. She hid the soap container under a carton of samples in the back of his closet. She removed his aspirin and vitamins from the vial and substituted the blood thinner pills. She put the vial back in his drawer and waited. I figured Lynnie put the vial of blood thinner medication in her desk either mistakenly or to frame Carrie, but I got it wrong. Carrie planted it in Lynnie's desk to frame Lynnie. Both Carrie and Lynnie planted the medication at Jack's house, hoping to implicate Mo Mac. Carrie's fingerprints were on the containers in the frig in Jack's garage. Snip said Jack drowned, but the thallium poisoning killed him. The amount of thallium in Jack's thermos the day he died could have killed an elephant." I widened my eyes. "It turns out Lynnie and Carrie hated each other as much as they hated Jack. So much so, they destroyed one another along with him. In the end, they succeeded beyond their wildest dreams." I shook my head. "Beats all, doesn't it? Two crazy women competing to kill the same guy and annihilate one another."

Joan mused, "So where was Carrie's big mistake?"

I swiped a napkin across my coffee cup. "She got sloppy and forgot to wipe her fingerprints off the vial. Her thumbprint on the top of the vial in Jack's house sealed her fate. The lab compared the fingerprint to the ones on my boat, and they matched." I grinned from ear to ear. "Her fingerprints were in the state system after she got arrested a few years ago in San Diego at an *animal rights protest*. Lady Justice might be blind, but she has one wicked sense of humor."

Chapter Thirty-Six

Gary Burkett, our head designer, fell in love with Mira Kumar's designs when Queenie and I took him on a tour of several stores featuring Mira's adorable line. After convincing David Mira is the perfect designer to fill the huge design gap in our product line, we enticed her to join forces with Mermaid once we promised she could still do her own thing. Much to our surprise and delight, she agreed.

Mira's first assignment was to create a capsule collection as a preview of next season's cruise line. At the end of Mira's flawless presentation, David, Gary, Queenie, and I gave her a standing ovation.

As the four of us headed out of David's office, the boss said, "Holly, a minute, please."

I took a seat across from him, and he peered at me over the rim of his glasses. "You do realize nothing has changed, right?"

I gave him the same you-must-be-crazy expression Siggie often gives me. "Surely you jest. Respectfully, *everything* has changed."

He rolled his eyes. "It's so unbecoming to play dumb."

Hey, nowhere is it written that I had to make it easy for him.

He pursed his lips. "Let me spell it out for you. You're still not keeping the juniors and kids divisions."

I scoffed. "Why not? It's not as if *your idea* worked out so great. From my seat in the bleachers, the phrase *nuclear bomb* comes to mind."

David flashed his patented nice try but no dice grin. "Forget it."

I poked the stick a bit further into the open wound and smirked. "Since you were *so successful* the last time, do you have another *outstanding candidate*?"

To my surprise, he burst out laughing. "Not a chance. This time *you're* gonna do the vetting."

My eyes widened. "So, if the next one's a clunker, it's on me."

His hands twirled into a ta-da motion. "Exactly."

I grinned evilly. "No problem. I've got the perfect candidate in mind. If the person has any interest in meeting with you, I'll set up the interview."

****

David and I concluded our meeting as Harvey Mazer walked into David's office. He hefted the small carton containing his personal belongings onto the corner of David's desk and put out his right hand. Harvey smiled sardonically. "I couldn't leave without saying goodbye."

"Harvey." David shook his head sadly as he grasped Harvey's hand. "There are no words to express how sorry I am for this. Jack Tyne was my bad, not yours. The board should have punished me, not you."

Harvey laughed out loud. "I'm sure old Earl Bernard agrees, but he's a practical man." Harvey patted David's fancy mahogany desk. "It's a whole lot easier to replace a lowly bean counter than it is the face of the company." Harvey shrugged. "Besides, he and the board blame me for the mess of things Jack made." Harvey poked a stubby index finger into the hollow of his chest. "I signed off on the separate sales, design, and merchandising teams, the separate design studio, the separate trade show portable booth, the separate sales meeting, and—" David winced as Harvey added, "And let's not forget the separate New York showroom and the fabulously unsuccessful, but pricey launch party. And to add insult to injury, I revised the budgets of other *profitable* divisions to accommodate all those things and submitted the budget to the board. I took funds away from other healthy divisions and funneled them into a bottomless money pit. At the end of the day, while you approved all those idiotic expenditures, plus the mountain of unsold fabric, I still should have stopped you, and I didn't." Harvey shrugged. "I failed to meet my responsibility to ensure company profitability, and it cost me my job."

David shook his head. "This is a mistake the board will regret making."

Harvey snorted. "Too bad the board doesn't think so."

David puckered his lips. "Do you have any job leads? Feel free to use me as a reference."

Harvey tapped David's wrist. "Appreciate the offer. No, not yet, but don't worry about me. I'll be fine. Bean counters always land on their feet." Harvey took off his eyeglasses and waved his specs at David in a warning. "You, my friend, are the one who should be looking over your shoulder. The scuttlebutt is the board is already searching for my replacement. I guarantee it won't be some wet-behind-the-ears newbie for you to intimidate and push around." Harvey pointed his fingers at David and made the motion of a gun. "The rumor is they're also creating a new position. Chief Operating Officer who answers to the board, and whose main function is to serve as a minder *specifically for you.*"

David grinned. "I better get ahead of the curve on this one. Guess I'm gonna need someone to watch my back."

Harvey rested his hand on my shoulder. "You already have one. The rest of us wrote you off as a stone-cold killer, but this one never wavered. She risked her career, and nearly lost her life to prove your innocence." Harvey squeezed my arm and grabbed his carton. He walked to the door and gave the boss a two-fingered salute. "Take care of yourself, David."

As Harvey disappeared, David mused out loud. "Trust me, I always do." David opened a copy of the *West Coast Apparel News* and thumbed through a few pages until he found a specific article. The headline read, *"No one's talking at Royal Swimwear. CEO Butch Oldham Out."* David flipped through his Rolodex and stopped at the letter O.

Before he dialed the number, David should have remembered that sometimes God punishes us by granting us our wishes. David will live to regret not following my nana's sage advice: Be careful what you wish for. You might get it. David crooned into the receiver, "Butch Oldham, please." David smiled like a shark. "Who's calling? Tell him it's his favorite protégé."

I locked eyes with David. He jutted his jaw defiantly but had the grace to blush as he pushed us all from the frying pan into the fire.

A word about the author...

Born in the Big Apple, award-winning cozy mystery author Susie Black now calls sunny Southern California home. Like the protagonist in her Holly Swimsuit Mystery Series, Susie is a successful apparel sales executive. Susie began telling stories as soon as she learned to talk. Now she's telling all the stories from her garment industry experiences in humorous mysteries.

She reads, writes, and speaks Spanish, albeit with an accent that sounds like Mildred from Michigan went on a Mexican vacation and is trying to fit in with the locals. Since life without pizza and ice cream as her core food groups wouldn't be worth living, she's a dedicated walker to keep her girlish figure. A voracious reader, she's also an avid stamp collector. Susie lives with a highly intelligent man and has one incredibly brainy but smart-aleck adult son who inexplicably blames his sarcasm on an inherited genetic defect.

Looking for more? Visit her website: http://www.authorsusieblack.com

Sign up for her reader list and receive a free swimwear fit guide.

Or reach her at mysteries_@authorsusieblack.com

Thank you for purchasing
this publication of The Wild Rose Press, Inc.

For questions or more information
contact us at
info@thewildrosepress.com.

The Wild Rose Press, Inc.
www.thewildrosepress.com